MW00974391

NAILED

by

Allan B. Thames

Edited by Carrie Thames McElroy

Text copyright ©2018 Allan B. Thames

All Rights Reserved

Abbott Authors

The goal of Abbott Authors is to
inspire. enlighten. entertain.
challenge. and comfort people
with our written and spoken
word

Cover photo taken by Rita Lacey Goode

DEDICATION

This book is dedicated to women who feel trapped in abusive situations, whether mental, emotional, verbal or physical. It is an encouragement to them that there is life beyond abuse.

It is also an encouragement to churches everywhere to go out to the highways, the hedges, the streets, the lanes, the trailer parks, the boarding homes, the slums, the inner city, the subdivisions of suburbia, to the retirement homes, nursing homes and assisted living facilities, to the rich and to the poor and everyone in between. We must not forget that there are people in need at our own back doors. The gospel has the power to change their lives.

FOREWARD
True Testimony by Adrienne Thames

2017 & 2018 have been very transformative years for me. For so long I have been afraid to tell my story. I thought I was protecting myself by avoiding to tell it, but in reality the only person I was protecting is someone I said I would never protect again. I started to let go of the shame I was holding onto and realized that God was going to use my story as soon as I found my voice to tell it. So here it is.

I grew up in the church. I was not just a "worship on Sunday kind of a girl", but someone who was 100% sold out for Christ. When I was 12 or 13, I spent my summer as a missionary in Germany. I have always had an extra big heart. I would go without in order to give to someone who I saw in need. I have always been a fixer, it is just who I am. Unfortunately, that meant many times in life I was taken advantage of and used. I am a 100% all or nothing kind of person. If it is worth doing, I am going above and beyond. I do not give up. Have you ever met someone who lit up a room just by walking in? The life of the party? The girl with the contagious smile? Someone who makes world a better place just by being in it? I was that person. I always saw the best in people or the potential that they have. I would give someone the shirt off my back or anything really if I thought they needed it. I walked with confidence. I loved who I was as a person. I knew what I had to offer and I was proud of who I was. I think it is important to explain who I was in order to understand the cost of what was lost for so long.

At the age of 17, the best friend of a guy that I was l seeing raped me. At the time I blamed myself for allowing myself to be in that situation. He took a piece of me that night that I will never get back. I was filled with emotions I had never felt before. I was disgusted and ashamed. I could not figure out how God could allow something like that to happen. If I had only known then what was coming. I turned my back on God at this point. My focus shifted from living a life focused on God, to living a life focused on myself and doing whatever I felt like doing. This led to lots of partying and hanging out with the wrong crowd. Deep down I still had the desire to help "fix" people which led to some fairly toxic relationships.

The first time I met him I should have known to run from his crooked smile. There was just something about him that I had to know more. He was the most charming person I had ever met, but somehow he had never had a girlfriend or serious relationship before. That should have been a red flag to me, but somehow it was just more of a challenge. He knew all the right things to say. I fell hard and I fell fast. I did not realize the control and manipulation had already begun. I was in love and I thought I was happy.

The first six months were amazing or so I thought, mostly because I did not know he was already sleeping with other women. I say already, but that would assume he ever stopped sleeping around in the first place which was highly unlikely. My children recently asked me about the first time he hit me, but it is not that simple. It did not happen suddenly all at once or I would have left. It started with manipulation, control, and verbal abuse. It was so gradual that I never saw it coming. He had this magical ability to blame everything on me and fully convince me that I actually was my fault. He somehow could talk his way out of anything. If I would confront him about a lie he was caught in, he would not only convince me it was not true, but would make me feel crazy for ever believing he could be in the wrong.

The first time he spit in my face something inside of me broke. I could see in his eyes that my brokenness somehow excited him, it became one of his favorite things to do. He degraded me in ways that I didn't even know were possible. I felt more and more worthless. As my confidence broke, he was able to convince me I was lucky to have him because no one else would want a worthless failure like me. The verbal and emotional abuse became a daily thing, somehow just part of my daily life. If I happened to have a moment of confidence he would break me back down anyway that he saw fit. I walked on eggshells trying to keep the abuse to a minimum. Something as simple as the dog spilling water in the kitchen or something happening at work could set him off. The physical abuse was escalating. What had started with him throwing something in anger and it accidently hitting me, had turned into pushing and shoving. The more he put his hands on me like that, it seemed the more he felt like a man. I was so scared of him at that point that I would not even fight back because I knew he would kill me. I could tell by the look in his eyes when he would wrap his hands around my neck that he was capable of it. He would watch the life start to leave my eyes as he choked me then let go so I could gasp for air. He would threaten that if I ever left him, he would hunt me down and finish me off for good. I learned how to put on a happy face because I could never let anyone know the truth. If I did, it would make him look bad and I would have to suffer the consequences. Honestly, I think part of it was also the fact that someone else knowing would make it a reality, then I could no longer live in the denial that I called home. The first time I was really going to leave, he proposed. He knew how much I wanted to get married so he used that to make me stay. It was always empty promises used only to meet his agenda. Somehow, I truly believed it was my fault. I just knew if I could be perfect everything would get better. If I could clean the house just right, cook the perfect meal, and make sure not to say anything stupid I thought it would get better each day. I was wrong. Nothing I ever did was good enough for him.

He made me feel like the most stupid person in the world. The things that he would call me turn my stomach now. He would break me down until I was the shell of a person laying on the floor sobbing. I have never been suicidal and I have never wanted to die, but there were moments of brokenness where I truly believed it would have been easier to be dead. Sometimes he would stand there holding a gun and I wondered why he never just pulled the trigger. I would be so hysterical I somehow would just go numb. I would stop feeling. Those were the moments he would bend me over the bed and do whatever he wanted to me regardless if I said stop. I wished I could just melt into the bed and disappear.

He began to isolate me from everyone I cared about. He needed all of my attention to be on him because if it was on someone else they might help me see the truth. He convinced me that all my family and friends were against him, that they were just trying to keep us from happiness. A cycle began. Things would get really bad so I would threaten to leave. He would make a grand gesture and convince me to stay, that things really were going to change. Things would seem amazing for a few days or a week, then it would all start to crumble again. I finally decided I was brave enough to leave and I found out I was pregnant. I stayed because I thought my child was better off with a mother and father. I felt like a failure in everything else already, how could I fail my unborn child also. I could take anything for my children. When I was about six months pregnant with my oldest, he fractured my ribs and ankle. He was kicking me out and as I had some of my stuff in bags to leave, he grabbed me by the neck and slammed me into the wall. I
slid down the wall on to a barrel his mother had by the door before finally falling to the ground.

As I army crawled out of his mother's house sobbing, his sister told me I needed to get up and leave. I had a couple friends take me to the emergency room and I told them my dog knocked me down the stairs. I would "hop" between ERs so that none would pick up on the abuse. Every time I went to a doctor they would ask me if I felt safe in my home. Every single time, I would lie.

If they knew the truth he would have killed me. I actually stayed away for a few months when he kicked me out that time. Yet he was able to convince me yet again that he changed and life would be good so I went back. Things actually went fairly well when my oldest was born. We were happier than we had been in a long time. My time was spent caring for my child, which just allowed him more time to do whatever or whoever he felt like on the side. Like always things started to crumble. Then I found out I was pregnant again. Even though I was four months pregnant, he tried to convince me to have an abortion. Someone said not to worry, we could find someone who would do it even though it was illegal in our state. When my second son was born things got a little better again, then they got worse. I was fully convinced I could take anything for my children. I thought I was doing what was best for them. Little did I know the damage had already started with them. When my oldest was two he would try to protect me from his dad. I wish I could say that when he would step in front of me that his father stopped screaming, but that was rarely the case. Thankfully, he never hurt the children which ironically was another reason I stayed as long as I did. Because it was my fault he was always angry not the children, so why should I take them away from their father? I really thought I was the problem.

I will never forget the moment it finally clicked that this was wrong and I needed to find a way out for us. I got a call in the middle of the night to come pick him up from the bar or he was going to be arrested. I loaded up my two small children into the car and drove to the bar. He was drunk and most likely high on something also. It took forever to get him in the car. When I was trying to drive home, he grabbed my phone and tried to throw it out the window. He then punched me in the face and jerked the wheel trying to run us off the road. My oldest who was three at the time started screaming, "Daddy's trying to kill us" over and over. I pulled over at one of his friend's houses and let him out of the car. He was standing in the yard as we pulled away.

I was not going to let him endanger my children. I had tears stinging my cheek where he had hit me as my oldest asked me something I will never forget, he said "Mommy what did you do that made daddy so mad?" I knew in that moment we had to find a way out. I had done nothing to deserve what his father had done to me.

It took a little time after that to finally have the courage to leave. He kicked me and the kids out like he had done so many times before. My mother drove twelve hours through the night to pick us up. He even

9

paid her gas money just so we would be gone. As we were getting ready to leave, he leaned in the car and said to my oldest, "You cannot see daddy anymore because mommy is bad." I wish I could say it was easy at that point, but for a couple months I desperately wanted to go back. When the abuse is that ingrained in you, their voice is still in your head long after they are gone. Somehow, in trying to survive the abuse you truly start to believe that you cannot live without them. Looking back, I believe the verbal and emotional abuse was worse than the physical. With the physical, the wounds start to heal immediately.

The emotional wounds last far beyond that and the emotional scars last forever. Whoever said sticks and stones may break my bones, but words could never hurt me has never experienced domestic violence and abuse. If they had, they would know the pain and destruction words can cause.

He broke me until I was a shell of a person. Over the years I had tried so hard to cope. I self medicated trying to numb myself. I blocked so much out. I thought I would never be able to trust another man. After a few months of healing the best I could, I woke up one morning and decided I would go to church with my mom. I had not been in so many years, but I knew if I was going to become whole again I needed to come to terms with God. That Sunday morning I had no intention of God leading me to join the church, but he laid it on my heart and I walked forward.

The way my mother ended up in that church is completely a God thing. My father had an aortic dissection, which means his aorta tore from inside his heart all the way down into his right leg. We were called back numerous times being told that he would not make it through the night. He was in multiple organ failure. During one of his many surgeries we were in the waiting room for the Cardiac ICU in downtown Atlanta. My mother, my sister, and myself were laughing at a story one of us had told. My family even in the hard times really knows how to laugh. A woman walked up to my mother and said she just had to know what we were laughing about. Her husband was having bypass surgery. She happened to live in the same area as my mother and invited her to church; the church that just happened to be across the street from her neighborhood.

After joining the church, I had been to a few church functions and Wednesday night bible
studies. At one of the bible studies during the prayer time, someone mentioned that we needed to pray for the mission trip, that several people had dropped off the team. I prayed and I said God if you want me to go, then please show me how to make it possible. That Friday I drove into Atlanta to the passport office and was able to renew it the same day and I was given two buddy passes. I was going to Mexico to build a house. I surrendered everything back to God, and asked him to use me as I was needed. That Sunday the mission team stood in front of the church and held hands as the elders prayed over our trip the next morning. The last thing I was expecting was that the man standing beside me, holding my hand as we were prayed over, would become my husband. We held hands before we even spoke to each other. Three short months later, he kneeled in that same spot we first held hands and proposed. Three more months later we were married a few feet from that spot. Before I met Ben, if you had told me I would know my husband for six months before marrying him I would have laughed. I would never have believed you can have such certainty in such a small amount of time, but God had a different plan. And when you know you know. As we celebrated our Sixth wedding anniversary this past May, I am even more confident in that fact that God provided me the man that my children and myself needed in our family.

As a wedding present to me, Ben was going to buy me a handgun. I am a bit of a gun fanatic. We went gun shopping I picked out the one I wanted. I tried to purchase the gun and I was told they had to do a more extensive background check for some reason. So I put a deposit on the gun to hold it and was contacted a few days later that I was denied. I had to write a letter to find out why I was denied. Imagine my surprise when I found I had a warrant out for my arrest in the state of VA for charges related to my ex, somewhere that I had left almost a year before at this point. Yet God provided a way for me to renew my passport when I never should have been able to. As soon as I found out, I immediately wanted to drive to VA to turn myself in, as they would not tell me the charges over the phone. My parents wanted to hire a lawyer first, but I told them that I had to take responsibility for my actions in the past. God had changed my life, but I still had to face the consequences I deserved. My father drove up to VA with me and I turned myself in. I was facing very serious felony charges. My father bonded me out and I had to return to VA for court not long after that. My lawyer showed the judge that I had completely changed my life when I moved and 2 of the charges were dropped. The third charge was reduced to a misdemeanor and I was given probation.

With that behind me, it helped bring me closure to turn the page and focus on my new family.   My husband and I were thrilled to find out we were pregnant early on in our marriage. Our older two boys were so excited for a new sibling to spoil. Unfortunately, we found out around 16 weeks that there was not a heartbeat. We would suffer one more miscarriage, before we got pregnant with Zade. We were cautious to get excited and my heart fell when I started cramping somewhere around 8 weeks. My husband took me to the Emergency Room and I cried silently as we waited for the bad news. The ultrasound tech asked if I knew anything about ultrasounds, which I was all too familiar with at this point. So I was overjoyed when she turned the screen to show me the little flicker of his heartbeat. We were blessed with his birth 4 weeks early, and you could not tell looking at him today that he had a 2-week NICU stay for respiratory distress. We have come through 7 more miscarriages since, but we are so thankful to be expecting our fourth
boy in February of 2019!

Around age 6 our middle child Neal was diagnosed with Asperger's/Autism Spectrum Disorder, Sensory Processing Disorder, and ADHD. He began to struggle in the public school. He became the child who banged his head against the wall and tied his shoes together.

I was scared to go more than 5 minutes away from the school because I never knew when I was going to get the call that I needed to come calm him down. My child's behavior was spiraling out of control and I felt like I was failing as a mother. My child had no friends. He had no confidence. He felt like he was stupid. My heart broke when after having to restrain him during a meltdown, he looked up at me with tears streaming down his face and he asked, "Why did God make me so bad?" We started daily affirmations with him trying to build his confidence and learned which techniques would help Neal center himself when he was "spinning". A church member had suggested we check out the Bedford Academy. After meeting with the director of the school I knew that was where Neal needed to be, but there was no way we could afford the tuition. We prayed that if this was God's will, he would show us the way to get Neal there and he moved mountains.

Within the first couple of weeks I saw a confidence that I had never before seen in my child. He was happy and excited to go to school. For the first time ever my 8 year old had friends at school. As we come to the end of the year, my child that I was scared would be kicked out of public school has had no behavior problems at Bedford at all. He has maintained straight A's the entire year and his behavior across the board has improved. It is incredible to see him truly happy.

Through all the ups and downs of our lives together, one thing that has never wavered was our passion for ministry. In 2016, we created Ignite, which is a gathering for young adults who are passionate about serving Jesus and coffee.

While I still have triggers and scars that will always be a part of me, I am thankful that I have once again found the girl that can light up a room just with a different kind of strength behind her. I may have turned my back on God, but he never turned his back on me. He was just waiting for me to let go and give it to him. He has given me this story so that I can help women in these situations. God has freed me from my past, and given me freedom not just to survive, but to thrive in him. I am free from the monsters in my past.

I hope you will read the following novel, not a real life story or true account of anyone's actual life, but perhaps a brief picture of the abuse that some women face and deal with every day.

Chapter One
"The Wrecker Towed My Love Away"

"An ear can break a human heart
As quickly as a spear,
We wish the ear had not a heart
So dangerously near."
Emily Dickinson

He never should have married her. He had known that since shortly after they had said the "I do's" and the "I will's" and sealed the vows with that now meaningless kiss. Nearing the end of that tumultuous nineteen-year marriage, Wallace Harris was emotionally drained. For almost every day of those past nineteen years, his soon to be ex-wife had found some way to hurt him, to not only dig the knife in but to twist it, too. Now the thing that Wallace feared more than an aching heart, loneliness, was about to become his constant companion. He did not want to live alone because he was terrified of dying alone. Their only child, Lauren, had found her own ways to inflict incredible pain on her father, the worst of which was the announcement that she had decided to live with her mother and her mother's boy toy, Roger. Lauren would be moving away to college in the fall anyway, but Wallace knew he was going to miss his final summer with her and that hurt, too.

Wallace should have been surprised by his wife's sudden announcement that she was seeking a divorce, but he wasn't. Divorce. Now there was a word he had hated since his own parents had divorced. He hated the word, hated the thought that he was getting divorced and even hated the song D-I-V-O-R-C-E. He knew and believed that divorce had never been part of God's master plan, yet he was being forced to go through it. Sadly, even though she had been raised in the church, Rachel Lynn had found a way to violate her marriage vows and avoid the guilt. Adultery and the biblical implications were subjects that she ignored as most people involved in it seemed to do. She simply refused to think about the future consequences. "Till death do us part" was more than just words to Wallace, however. If they hadn't been, he would have left her years ago.

Standing just under six feet tall, weighing 189 lbs., which was the most he had ever weighed in his life, Wallace (or Wally as some chose to call him but always a name he had hated) had an ever expanding bulge around his waist. When he looked in the mirror he felt almost ninety years old, seeing his brown, thinning hair now liberally sprinkled with gray reflecting back at him, having been surprised one day to see his old father's face in the mirror before him. Wallace had no hope of ever finding someone to marry him now since he certainly wouldn't want the person who would settle for him, a balding, graying, slow, fat man with more wrinkles on his face than money in the bank. When thinking about money, Rachel Lynn's credit card balance was another of her many secrets that he was just afraid to ask about because he suspected that a maxed out credit limit was another reason she was leaving. Along with her hair that was still as dark brown as when he had met her, she also had a gorgeous tanning salon sprayed-on tan. Rachel Lynn would be marrying this Roger whom he suspected had a similar sprayed-on tan and perfect hair. Wallace did not know him and did not want to know him, but he could almost bet that he had some kind of exotic car because Rachel Lynn had always been attracted to men with new or fast cars. Wallace had only won her attention when he drove up in a shiny blue and white 1969 Chevrolet Camaro with glass pack mufflers that you could hear coming a mile away. He had loved that car. Unfortunately, she had wrecked it in their second week of marriage. As the wrecker towed the totaled car away, he knew it was also towing away her love. He couldn't afford anything more than a beat up four door sedan he had found in a used car lot. When he drove that car up in the yard she simply walked around it once, then went inside without ever saying a word.

Sometimes Wallace felt like he was living a country western song that no one could ever believe. 'My Baby Wrecked My Hot Rod So The Wrecker Towed My Love Away.'

Rachel Lynn, and she was always called Rachel Lynn and not ever Rachel, nor Lynn, as if it were written "Rachellynn", had already left a trail of broken hearts behind her when she met Wallace, having been engaged twice before she graduated High School. When she had seen his car drive up in the mall parking lot, she did not care what kind of man got out of it, she was going to marry him because she loved that car. Before the evening was out a very flirtatious Rachel Lynn had coaxed Wallace into taking her home, (and into driving very fast on that ride), into asking her out on a date, and before the month was over she had talked Wallace into asking her to marry him. Anybody who could drive that car had to be a real man, a man that could provide for her and give her newer cars and faster cars. She didn't know it had taken Wallace almost his whole life savings to buy that Camaro. When she found that out she was already pregnant she had to tolerate the situation, but she never forgave Wallace for that old, dented, worn out, embarrassing sedan.

Rachel Lynn noticed the 'spare tire' around Wallace's middle. She noticed his increasingly flabby arms. She noticed his thinning hair and noted his refusal to dye it. Wallace was aging right before her eyes but she, however, was not going to have anything to do with aging or any old people if she could possibly help it. He could grow old if he wanted, but not with her. For his part, Wallace noticed that many times Rachel Lynn would flirt with Lauren's boyfriends and would often dress in Lauren's clothes. It was as if she was living her teenage years all over again through Lauren. He believed Rachel Lynn had never matured mentally beyond her teens. Wallace was not a philosopher or psychologist, but he had come to the conclusion that some people like Rachel Lynn reached a certain level of maturity and never grew beyond it. For Rachel Lynn, she was eternally a teenager. Or wanted to be.

The cold, dreary day in February finally came when the dreaded divorce was final, the chill in the air matching the frost on his heart. Wallace hated being alone, but now he seemed to be assured that he would be alone for a long time to come. As they walked out of the courthouse, Wallace noticed a brand new behemoth of a sport utility vehicle, a real gas sucker, waiting at the curb. A smiling Rachel Lynn sailed past Wallace without a word and into the huge tank. It drove away with a squeal of the tires and a laugh from Rachel Lynn that seemed as if it were aimed at her now ex-husband. When Wallace got home he learned from Lauren what he had suspected, that the SUV was Roger's, 'one of his toys'. Rachel Lynn was another one of his toys. Roger and Rachel Lynn were dashing off to get married so Wallace knew now that Roger had been 'plowing with his heifer before he had even unhitched it.'

Once again, he felt the hurt that had been growing as he had faced today's final proceedings. Now he seemed less a man, a man that had not been able to satisfy his wife, a man that had driven his wife into another's arms, a man whose own daughter was soon to leave him to live with her mother. He was a failure. Totally. Not only that, when Lauren left next week, he would be a lonely failure. Lauren had plunged one dagger into his heart, but Rachel Lynn had twisted hers. Julius Caesar would have felt the same daggers on that infamous ides of March.

Chapter Two
Broken Heart

***"What therefore God hath joined together, let not man put asunder. "*Jesus Christ**

"God," the Reverend William Deveraux Lee intoned loudly to his congregation, "is no respecter of persons." Several "Amens" bounded up to him. It was like throwing gas on a fire as his voice grew deeper and louder. "God never chooses those we would choose to do his work. God looks not at the outside of a man. God looks at the heart!" Amen after amen rippled from the congregation.

Reverend William Lee was a spirit-ignited ball of fervor and John the Baptist flame. Claiming to be a proud direct descendent of Civil War General Robert E. Lee, he believed that the Lord had called him to the pulpit and to the ministry. Part of that ministry involved winning people to that Lord, and that included the waitresses at his favorite restaurant, what all the locals just called "The Barn". Leading them, and others, to the Christ he served epitomized what being in the ministry was all about, seeking the lost wherever they might be found. Arriving at the Waffle Barn every Saturday morning at sunrise, the preacher sat at his usual table with a cup of coffee at his right hand, his Bible and study guide in front of him, and a plate full of eggs and bacon just to his left. He spent many a cholesterol-filled hour hunched over the eggs as he drew deeper meanings from the scripture he had studied all week, meanings he would impart to the church members the next day, and maybe even to the waitress if she gave him the opportunity. He tipped really well, which all the waitresses knew, so they usually did not mind listening to him try out one of his main sermon points on them. "Reverend Will" as he was called by some ("I'm The Will of God", he often joked, "and Gracie, my wife, is 'The Grace of God'"), looked like a Marine. Tall, muscular, intimidating with penetrating eyes that reflected out of a soul that knew its mission

in life, when he preached it was like a boot camp drill instructor
exhorting his recruits, but with cleaner, non-profane words. Not a man
to be trifled with, he was not afraid to let his church board of deacons
know how he felt in meetings where he usually got his way. There
was some hushed talk about him having been a bar room bouncer
before he found the Lord, but no one dared ask him about that because
that was in a shadowy God forgiven past.

Reverend Will did not know everyone in town, but he knew everyone
that mattered, which meant to him that he knew everyone for whom he
might do a favor in exchange for a favor somewhere down the road.
He did not mind going out of his way for people because he
understood one of the maxims of life that his dad had taught him. "Be
nice to people on the way up, because you might need them on the
way back down." Also, he did not mind having people owe him
favors since he was never shy about cashing in on them. John
Shoemake, the funeral home director, owned a cabin on a local lake
and had a nice fishing boat to go with it. Reverend Will helped him
out several times by doing funerals for folks who didn't have a
minister and could not afford one so an appreciative John repaid him
by letting him use the cabin and fishing boat on occasion. And Will
did love to fish. The joke was that he named the boat *Visitation*, and if
a church member ever called wanting to know where he was, his wife
could truthfully answer "out on *Visitation*."

Will also was a good friend of the local supermarket manager. For
running free ads in the church newsletter, and mentioning the store
from the pulpit once in a while, Will was entitled to his pick of the
choicest steaks whenever he wanted. The minister had this type of
deal with several town merchants, but especially with those who were
members of his congregation. You could call him any time, day or
night, and he would come running. When he wanted or needed
something, you would gladly do the same.

Reverend Will was also a master psychologist. He did not have the
school training or the degree, but he had mastered in watching people,

learning from them and understanding what made them tick. From a five-minute conversation he usually could glean all the information he needed to determine just exactly how he could appeal to that person or how that person could be useful to him or his ministry. He had known Rachel Lynn in high school, and had dated her several times when he got his first car, a very fast Pontiac GTO. She had left him when the transmission of the car did. Some guy in a shiny, Dodge Charger won her attention soon after that. Reverend Lee also knew before her husband did that she was messing around with another man. He knew something was seriously wrong when Wallace started coming to church without her. At first, the excuse was she had to work, then she was sick, then no excuses at all were offered. When he had seen her at the store, she had turned quickly away to avoid him. Not long after that word had come of the pending divorce. Wallace had come in for counseling but Rachel Lynn had never come either with or without him. A bitter Wallace had quit the counseling when he finally realized the marriage was broken.

Sitting in his office late one evening trying to catch up on his weekly sermon preparation because he had "snuck off and gone fishing with a couple of the deacons on *Visitation*", Preacher Will Lee's phone rang.

"Hey, man", he called loudly and cheerfully into the phone when he heard Wallace Harris's voice. "I haven't seen you around church in a while. You know you shouldn't sneak off and go fishing without inviting me."

There was a momentary silence as Wallace struggled to keep the emotion he was feeling out of his voice. "Hey, Reverend. No, not fishing though sometimes I wish I could get away from it all and go again. Well, you know about the divorce. I just called to let you know that it was finalized today. Then I heard that Rachel Lynn was getting married right afterwards, and Lauren is going to live with her." There was a momentary pause. "So it has been kind of a rough day."

Reverend Lee could feel the man's hurt and sighed deeply. "I am so sorry. What kind of car does her new fellow have?"

That brought a laugh from the man on the other end of the line and the minister was glad to hear it. "Well, it's a brand new SUV. Big vehicle. Everybody who is anybody has one, but I'm a nobody, so I don't. Now Rachel Lynn has one so I guess she is finally somebody. She's always wanted to be a somebody."

"I don't have one either. But Rachel Lynn was always that way. She's always judged her men by the car they drive. If you hurry out and buy a Jaguar this week I guarantee she will come running back to you." He was trying to be light hearted. When he heard no answer, he continued in a more serious vein. "You can't let Rachel Lynn ruin your life. You still have your life to live. You have to go on. There are other women out there who will love you for who you are. Divorce never has been God's way, but man, or woman in this case, has made it their way."

"I don't know, Preacher." There was a definite sadness in the voice. "I'm damaged goods. Not only damaged goods, but aging damaged goods. I don't think any decent woman my age would look at me twice. Besides that, I'm struggling to keep the house going with just me there. It's a mess right now. That was another issue Rachel Lynn had with me. She believes in "a place for everything and everything in its place" while I just kind of let things fall where they may and stay there. So I'm a loser all the way around."

"Don't think like that, man!" The Reverend Will Lee always detested hearing a defeatist attitude. "Listen to me. What man and woman tear apart, God can put back together. Maybe Rachel Lynn has destroyed your marriage, but she will have to live with the consequences and there are always consequences. I believe God is going to bring someone else into your life that is going to make you forget all about Rachel Lynn, somebody that needs you in their life. In fact, I am going to start praying just that."

The next words from Wallace Harris formed an unexpected question. "If God cares so much for me, then how come he let Rachel Lynn leave me? Why couldn't he make her still love me? I don't want anybody else. I want Rachel Lynn. Despite everything, I still love her. I always will. Isn't that the way it's supposed to be, the way God wants it? "

Will Lee sat at the desk and shook his head at the question he himself wrestled with often. "If God is so good, then why do bad things happen to good people?" "Wallace," he finally answered. "It is God's will that you and Rachel Lynn be together, but that is not Rachel Lynn's will. On this earth man's or woman's will seems to reign supreme. God is not going to force people to do things they refuse to do. We have free will. Bad things happen because God's will hasn't been totally achieved since the Garden of Eden."

Wallace was tired and didn't need a sermon. "Thanks, Preacher. You just keep praying for me and we'll see if God decides to do anything in my situation. I hate being lonely, but I hate to hurt like this, too."

"I really do understand." The minister finished the conversation with a quick prayer and Wallace promised to see him in church on Sunday. As he hung up, Reverend Will Lee turned his thoughts to his sermon and knew that he would have to deal with the issue of why good people suffer so much.

Chapter Three
Rescue

"The world is a dangerous place to live; not because of the people who are evil, but because of the people who don't do anything about it."

Albert
Einstein

Her feet were hurting terribly near the end of her twelve-hour shift at the Waffle Barn. Two of the other girls hadn't come in on this dreadfully rainy and cool Sunday, so she was working from 6:00 a.m. to 6:00 p.m. There had not even been time for a break at the most popular restaurant in town. Even though she was tired, she knew that with the tips she had made she would be able to pay her rent for the month. If all the stingy church people whom she had served that day had tipped at least 10%, she would have had enough to buy plenty of groceries for once. Elizabeth MacIntosh, called "Mac" by her closest friends, knew from experience that Sunday's were the worst tip days because the Christians might say they gave the Lord 10%, but not waitresses. She doubted very much that they gave the Lord his tithe either.

Just twenty-six years old but looking to some friends like she was going on forty, Liz or Lisa or Eliza as others called her, felt every one of those twenty six years this evening. Ever since her birth doctor held her naked little body upside down and slapped her bare bottom so sharply that her first breath was an agonizing cry, Mac had been a victim of men who seemed to take delight in hitting her or slapping her around. Her father, who professed to be a good, church going

Christian but was secretly a slave to the bottle, started hitting her before she could walk. It was truly amazing that her little pug nose had never been broken. After her father died suddenly when she was six, there was a series of her mother's boyfriends, and then several stepfathers, who carried on the almost ritualistic drinking to excess then hammering on Mac. When she turned thirteen, the budding young woman began going through boyfriend after boyfriend, most of whom were immediately dumped when they started hitting her. She had determined that she was not going to live the abusive life of her mother, but as she grew older, it seemed her boyfriends were all too much like her father. It was enough to make her few friends wonder if she was trying to satisfy some inner need by finding her father again in her boyfriends.

Hard living and the tough years of too many beatings had begun to take their toll on her face as the too many early wrinkles testified. Her cheekbones were sharp and obvious, while her chin was blunt from having stopped too many blows before they reached her nose. Short and thin, she was like a flower that sprouts up only to wither from lack of water and attention. Her naturally blond hair was cut perpetually short so that she would never have to bother about combing it or paying to 'have her hair done'. Slumping shoulders indicated her total disregard for herself or for anyone else. She was not really living, just existing, barely, and that was all. Life held neither joy nor meaning for her because life for her was about getting from day to day and nothing more.

Elizabeth MacIntosh was not only poor, but dirt poor as some would say. Having graduated near the bottom of her high school class due more to a lack of effort than a lack of intelligence, she did not go to college or pursue any kind of secondary education or training because she could not afford it and because she had no dreams, which more education could help her achieve. She had never been encouraged by her mother in any of her endeavors or in any part of her life since she was just another mouth to feed. After high school, Mac had drifted from job to job and relationship to relationship. Her latest boyfriend,

Harley Martin, was a very good motorcycle mechanic who many said was meaner than a snake and a man you didn't want to make mad. She feared him, but she feared what life would be without the little stability he offered. It would likely be a life of living in the woods with other homeless women she knew, or worse. Fear was her prime motivation for staying with him. She feared to be with him, but feared being without him even more.

She punched her time clock right at 6:00 p.m. with a sigh of relief. Her clothes smelled of bacon and coffee so her only uniform would have to be washed and ironed before she returned to work at 6:00 a.m. the next morning. Mac exited the rear door and walked around to the front of the building where Harley was supposed to be waiting, hopefully in his truck and not on his motorcycle. He was not there and that really irritated Mac, her blond hair now damp in the still falling drizzle. Ignoring the wet sidewalk, she sat down anyway to rest her feet and then leaned over to place her head in her lap.

Hearing an embarrassed cough behind her she looked up to find a middle-aged man staring down at her. She remembered having served him a few minutes earlier. "You left before I could tip you," he said. He was holding out a $5 bill.

"My shift was over," she said suspiciously. "If you want change you will have to go inside. I don't carry cash with me."

"Oh, no." The man looked concerned. "You did a great job even though I know you must be really tired. Yours was the first smile I've seen all day. And you took time to show you cared. I just wanted to thank you for it."

"No fooling?" She reached for the bill. She needed every dollar she could get her hands on, especially if Harley came looking for money to buy his nightly beer allotment. This $5 might just keep him from smacking her a time or two.

"No, no fooling." The man stood there stupidly not knowing what to do next.

"Well, thanks," the waitress said. "That's the nicest thing anyone has said to me in a long, long time." She smiled again, and so did the man.

There was another long silence as neither seemed to know how to end the conversation. Finally the man spoke. "Do you need a ride somewhere? I'm not a pervert or anything and I'm not trying to pick you up, but I can take you home if you need."

The young waitress gave him a wary look.

He hurriedly tried to explain further. "I hope someone would be able to help my daughter, Lauren, if she ever needed it. Maybe I'm paying it forward to the day she does need it and I'm not around anywhere."

Elizabeth MacIntosh was cautious. She had heard horrible stories of women getting picked up like this and being found murdered, if found at all. Somehow, she realized that like so many other areas in her life, she just didn't care anymore. Besides, where was Harley? It would serve him right to get there and find out she had already left. If she was found murdered, then he would be a suspect and that would teach him, too. Tired in body and soul, she started to stand and he offered his hand. She reached up and let him help her. "Okay," she said. "Sure. No problem."

"All I've got is this beat up, old sedan over there. I hope you don't mind riding in it. It is clean and dependable, if nothing else." Rachel Lynn's stinging criticism of it was still too fresh in his memory.

Mac followed his pointing hand to a dented car. "Looks like a Rolls Royce to me," she laughed, and the laugh felt good. In fact, every one of the two minutes or so she had spent with this stranger had felt good. He was a nice man, or at least so it seemed on the surface. She got in

28

the car and noticed the interior was spotless. "I live down in Sunny Valley Trailer Park," she offered. "You know where it is?"

"Go there every day," the man joked with a laugh. "Not really," he then said truthfully. "But if you point me in the right direction, then I'm sure we can find it. My name is Wallace by the way."

"Well, Mr. By the Way," Mac returned smartly, "turn right here out of the lot and straight on till I tell you to turn left over the tracks."

Wallace laughed. "I'm sorry, my name is Wallace Harris."

"Mine's Elizabeth MacIntosh. People call me Mac or Lisa or Liz, but I hate Eliza."

"Swell," Wallace said happily as he turned into traffic. "I will call you Elizabeth then."

"Just Elizabeth will work fine. No 'Then' to it."

Wallace laughed again. "Okay, 'Just Elizabeth'." He found her sense of humor delightful. A few minutes later, despite his trying to go slow and make his time with this girl last, she said "Turn left here." As he turned and crossed the train tracks he saw the sign for the trailer park, wondering why these areas always were "over the tracks"? The sign was bright, freshly painted, and encouraging. They turned in and she directed him to her trailer. Most of the trailers they passed looked nice in the dark with small, well-kept yards but a few of the others were cluttered with junk and looked deserted. These were the homes, Elizabeth explained, of the well-known drug dealers, homes which most of the trailer park tenants avoided because nothing good ever came out of them. Mac's was the smallest trailer in the complex, not that any of them were large. It was streaked with rust from the roof, its original color no longer discernable while dead weeds still stood in the yard where they had overtaken the vain attempt at a flower bed the summer before. As they pulled up and stopped, Elizabeth hesitated.

"Thanks Mr. By the Way. It's been a long day." She made no effort to get out.

"Is there something wrong?" Wallace asked, noting her reluctance to leave.

"Well, my boyfriend was supposed to pick me up at The Barn and when he finds out someone else brought me home, he's going to come over here and cause trouble. I kind of depend on him to get me back and forth to work."

Wallace was stunned. He lived in a middle class neighborhood, made a middle class salary, and had never really associated with those in any other class. The thought flashed through his mind that his church mission trips needed to be coming to places like this and not to places so far away like Mexico. There was so much poverty in their own backyard if they would just stop ignoring it. While his budget was often tight, he never missed paying a bill, even with Rachel Lynn's spending. This was his first trip into a trailer park and it was not a positive experience. He knew that many trailer parks were nice, this having been one of the nicer ones at one time, but now its age had begun to show and a seedy element had begun to take root. "You need me to call the police or something?" He was totally at a loss as to what to do.

"No!" she said emphatically. "I will manage."

She opened the door, but Wallace gently touched her arm. "I've got an idea. I've got a lot of room at my house. My wife just divorced me and moved her and my daughter out. You could spend the night there. I promise I won't touch you," he said quickly in response to her raised eyebrows. "You can stay in my daughter's room. It's still got the bed. Lock the door, too, if you want." The idea just rushed out of him. What a foolish notion.

Mac hesitated. Inside the tiny trailer was nothing but a bed, bathroom and a used, rickety couch left there by previous residents. It stank from what she didn't like to think. She had never been able to keep the roaches out and lately thought she heard rats trying to gnaw their way in. She hated rats. And she was afraid of Harley. "Thank you," she finally said. "You've done enough already. I think I could trust you but I won't have a way to get to work tomorrow."

"No problem there," Wallace said. "My dad has a truck he doesn't drive. I can borrow it." He hoped he wasn't being pushy.

She was very embarrassed. "I couldn't do that, Wallace. I really couldn't."

"I don't mind. I'm insured."

Mac shook her head. "You don't understand. I don't have a driver's license."

"Oh." Wallace was shocked. He had never met anyone her age that did not have a driver's license. "Well, what time do you have to be there?"

"6:00 a.m. It's going to be a short night."

Not knowing why, Wallace persisted. "Look, I usually leave the house at 6:00. Tomorrow morning I could leave a few minutes early. I will drop you off at The Barn. Maybe I will stop in for a cup of coffee. Problem solved."

Suddenly, Mac felt light hearted. "Okay," she said. "Let me run in and get my things. I will be right back. But keep the car running just in case Harley comes looking for me." It was a daring thing to do, but hanging around with a drunken, angry Harley was a daring thing to do every day. She decided to take a Wallace she did not know over the Harley that she did.

A few minutes later the young woman was back in the car bringing the smell of bacon back with her. She carried a solitary brown paper bag. "Home, James!" she chirped gaily as they pulled out of the park. They drove off into the dark, she hoping he was not a rapist and he hoping she was not a murderess.

Chapter Four
Is This Heaven?

"Wine is a mocker and beer a brawler; whoever is led astray by them is not wise." **Proverbs 20:1 NIV**

At ten minutes after six, a frustrated Harley Martin finished off another beer and looked at his watch, cursing lightly because he knew that he had once again left Mac waiting. She did hate to wait. He sat there for another couple of minutes before finally pulling himself to his feet as his long, dirty hair fell to his shoulders, covering the tattoo of a witch that stretched across his back from shoulder to shoulder. A week's growth of a weak beard dirtied his weak chin. Fishing for his truck keys in his faded blue jeans pocket, he finally stepped out into the rainy evening grumbling because if it weren't for the beer money he would just let her walk home like he had done before. He began to think that maybe he needed to talk to Freddy about raising her rent. That would be more money in his pocket, too.

A few minutes later he drove by the front of the Waffle Barn expecting to find Mac waiting in the mist. He knew she would get in cursing, but he also knew she might have some good tip money that he could use for more beer. Not seeing her at the usual spot, he drove through the lot several more times getting angry now because if she was working overtime she should have let him know. He finally stopped, getting out of the truck to go inside to ask the cashier where Mac was. Finding out she had left promptly at 6:00 p.m. when the shift ended, he stormed out and soon was roaring back to the trailer park. As he turned in, he noticed a dark sedan pulling out, but he did not look to see who was in it. He drove up to her trailer and saw it was dark. "Then let her walk home," he said, again cursing. "It'll serve her right. But I'm gonna make her pay when I see her again. I'll nail her hide to the wall if she's late again."

As they left the trailer park, Mac noticed the truck pulling in and ducked quickly. "That's Harley," she said, uttering an oath that made Wallace blush. "Get us out of here." Wallace accelerated quickly and was proud of how his car responded. Even Rachel Lynn would have been surprised at the speed the old car was making. After a few moments, Mac looked back. "That was close. Too close, but we missed him. Thanks."

Wallace slowed down and looked over at the young woman trying to make out her features in the dark. She was not beautiful, as he had noticed when she served him at The Barn, but she was attractive in her own way, or would be if given an extreme makeover like on television. "No," he admitted to himself, "Not beautiful, but still cute even without a makeover." He said nothing as he continued to drive through the dark.

Finally nearing Wallace's neighborhood, Mac spoke. "So where do you live?"

"In a subdivision just down the road here. The house was new when my wife and I moved in. It's almost nineteen years old now. Needs a little work, but it's comfortable. It's messy at the moment, though. I'm not the best housekeeper." They turned into his neighborhood with houses all in the $190,000 range. Not large by the standards of the day, but not small either. His house was a 3 bedroom, 2 bath, split level. When they drove up in the yard, Mac whistled.

"You didn't tell me you lived in a mansion!" She was amazed by the size.

"It's hardly a mansion." Wallace was pleased by her compliment. "It's just an average home."

"Average to you maybe," Mac snorted. "You got a butler, too?" She was beginning to wonder if she could be comfortable here in this opulence.

"Sure," Wallace laughed. "I've got a butler and his name is Wallace, but I've given him the night off. The maid and cook, whose names also happen to be Wallace, take Sunday's off, too. So the place is a little messy."

"Okay," said Mac as she got out of the car. "But it is still big, especially when compared to my little trailer."

Wallace reddened when he led Mac inside and saw the condition that the living room was in, with the Sunday paper strewed around, several shirts hanging on the sofa, and other things in disarray. He was glad he didn't have unfolded laundry, like his underwear, lying around but if the young waitress noticed the mess, she did not mention it.
Still amazed at how large the home was, the cathedral ceiling with the exposed beams awed her. "You got mice or rats?" she asked matter-of-factly.

He shook his head. "No, no rats or mice. Just a stray soon-to-be-dead roach once in a long while." He led her down the hallway to the right to his daughter's bedroom. "This is Lauren's room," he said. "You can sleep in here tonight. The bathroom is just across the hall. Towels are under the sink."

Mac was looking forward to a hot bath. "You got plenty of hot water? It would be great to get a bath to soak my feet. I need to wash my uniform, too."

"Sure," said Wallace. "Plenty of hot water. Help yourself. The washing machine is down the hall to the left, off the living room. I don't think I have any clothes left in there."

"Okay," said Mac, thoroughly uncomfortable that she found herself in a huge home with a man she did not even know. But she would be able to have a hot bath, wouldn't have to worry about mice or rats, and wouldn't have to worry about Harley, at least for one night. She didn't think she would have to worry about her host's motives either.

As she was putting her uniform in the washing machine, Wallace appeared with his phone in his hand. "You like pizza?" he asked.

"Yeah, I guess. Why?"

"I thought I would order some for supper. You hungry?"

The truth was she was famished. Back at the trailer she would have had a cheese sandwich on old bread. Pizza would be heavenly.

"You got any beer to go with that?" she asked.

"Sorry," said Wallace. "No beer."

"You don't drink do you?" asked Mac. She was disappointed because she thought a beer sure would have been good with pizza.

"No, Sorry. Don't smoke either."

"Figures," laughed Mac. "I get carried away to heaven and can't drink or smoke. Suddenly it ain't so heavenly. But, hey, I ain't goin to complain."

"Well, why don't you go ahead and get your bath while we are waiting on the pizza. It will take about thirty minutes or so to get here. They are busy tonight."

"That's one luxury I've never afforded," she said in wonder. "I dated a pizza delivery guy once, but he never brought me pizza. Not once."

An hour later, Elizabeth was sitting on the sofa with her feet propped up, a cold tea at her side and a lap full of steaming pepperoni pizza. Her hair was still wet from the bath as she sat there in the only pair of short pants she owned and a long t-shirt. Wallace was sitting in his big easy chair, sipping on tea, and sneaking a quick peek at his guest every now and again as she hungrily ate her supper. They were watching a basketball game on television which seemed to mesmerize the young woman. Wallace noticed that she looked far different, younger and more vulnerable, out of her uniform.

When she finished eating she got up and took her dishes to the kitchen where he heard her washing them. When she returned she yawned even though it was still early. Her host jumped up. "Can I get you anything?"

She laughed. "Just settle down, Mr. Wallace. I'm fine. No, I'm more than fine. I feel like I have died and gone to heaven. I've had a hot bath, a hot supper, and can sleep tonight without worrying about rats or roaches. I really do feel like I've died and gone to heaven, but I can't barely keep my eyes open. Would you mind if I went on to bed?"

"No. Whatever. You know where the room is." She walked over to him and kissed him quickly on the cheek before fleeing quickly up the hall to her bedroom. It reminded him of how his daughter used to kiss him goodnight.

Wallace sighed deeply wondering what he had gotten himself into in trying to help someone in distress. A few minutes later, bored by the ballgame, he turned the television off and locked up for the night, turning the burglar alarm on as usual. His room was just down the hall from the young waitress, so he quietly went into his room closing his door behind him. A few minutes later he was lying comfortably on the bed watching the dusty television that sat on his dresser. An old John Wayne western was on as Wallace drifted in and out of sleep.

Suddenly he jerked up as there was a knock on his door. Jumping up, he went over to open it. The small waitress stood there sleepily, with her pillow clutched to her chest. "This may sound crazy," she said, "but do you mind if I lay in here a while. I ain't trying to seduce you or anything, but I heard the movie on and thought I could watch it with you. Seems that I'm tired, too tired to sleep. I hate when that happens." The wild, unrealistic thought that Harley might find her in the night had unnerved her. Like a small child, she was afraid to sleep alone in this strange place.

Wallace shrugged his shoulders, a little uncomfortable with the idea of having this strange woman in his bed. She was surely taking a chance with him. He was surprised at the level of trust that had so quickly developed between them. "You like John Wayne?"

"My favorite," she said meaning it.

"Then climb aboard," he said. "The right side is mine, though."

She threw her pillow on the other side of the bed and soon was lying quietly beside him watching the movie. When a commercial came on, she asked a question that had been bothering her. "So why did you pick me up tonight? Think you could take advantage of me?"

Wallace shook his head, saddened by the suspicions that the world had forced onto people. "No. Nothing like that. I just thought I might be able to help you out. That's all. No ulterior motive. You looked like you needed a hand. The Bible says we are supposed to help each other, so I wanted to help."

"I mighta known you were a Bible thumper," she yawned. "Born again, saved and all that stuff. Just don't go trying to get me saved."

Wallace smiled to himself as the movie came back on. This girl had challenged even the purest of motives. "I won't," he promised, "though I might ask you to go to church with me sometime."

"So you were just being a Good Samaritan tonight when you picked me up." In her limited church experience she had heard about the Good Samaritan. Wallace had certainly been that this evening.

"Something like that I guess. What about tomorrow?"

"What about it? You are taking me to work right?"

"Yeah, but what about after that? Won't that Harley fellow give you problems?"

"Now, that ain't your worry, Saint Wallace. You let me handle Harley."

"Well," Wallace struggled for the right words to the idea that had been growing in his mind, "I'm in kind of a tough spot here myself. My wife is gone, and I am struggling trying to keep this house going, cleaning and cooking for myself, taking care of all the business. To be very truthful, I hate being alone."

"Welcome to the real world, but where are you going with this?" She had turned onto her side and was propping on her elbow as he lay on his back.

"Just an idea. I've got so much room here and you could use a better place to live. It sounds like you need to stay away from that guy."

"You askin' me to move in or marry you?" Her eyes were bright and twinkled as she understood immediately what Wallace was trying to ask.

"Well, why not move in? I won't charge you any rent, and you could pay your way by taking care of the house and doing laundry and stuff. I would help you get a driver's license and you could start driving my Dad's truck."

She flipped over on her back and put her arms behind her head and yawned again. "It sounds like its' too good to be true. There must be a catch somewhere. I'm sure I'll wake up in the morning and find out this has all been a dream, that I'm really Cinderella, but we'll talk about it later." With that, she fell quiet and before too many minutes had passed, she was breathing heavily. Wallace turned the television off and then rolled over onto his right side, being very careful not to touch the young stranger beside him. What had he gotten himself into? This was beyond strange and beyond believable.

What had she gotten herself into? Waking in the early morning hours, Mac was disturbed for the moment with the sound of someone snoring lightly beside her. She almost sat up in fright until she remembered where she was. She relaxed. That was something she did very seldom, even while sleeping. It was difficult trying to sleep while keeping a wary eye out for anyone that might come sneaking into her trailer to rob her, and for those pesky roaches and mice that she just couldn't keep out. For some reason, she trusted this strange man completely. What was there about him that comforted her, that helped her sleep without fear for the first time in years even though in the same bed with him? She hadn't even known him for twelve hours, and in fact, did not even know him at all. For whatever reason, she had decided to trust him.

How had she ever gotten into such a sorry state of life? It was a sorry state, a state she had promised herself never to get into, a state of having a drunk boyfriend who hammered on her. She had the scars, both physical and emotional, to prove it. Just like her mother. Mac had always wondered why her mother had never seemed to have a boyfriend who was normal, who was sober, and who wouldn't hit her. Now she knew. Mac was living her mother's life all over again, a life that her mother had certainly modeled for her, a life of learned helplessness, as the psychologists would say. At first Mac had wanted to live a successful life, dreamed of living in the suburbs, of being a happily married wife and mother, of being a soccer mom, of being respectable. Instead, she was the girlfriend of a mean drunk, living in

40

poverty, barely existing from day to day, her total possessions amounting to something less than $100. Need had driven her into Harley's arms, a man that feasted on vulnerable women like her. Mac did not like to think what she would do if he ever broke off their relationship. A tear came to her eye as she considered some of her friends who had been kicked out by their boyfriends and then just disappeared from society, at least the society that she knew. What kind of work they ended up in, she did not want to even consider. While having Harley as a boyfriend kept her away from that, she did not like to think what life would be like two years from now if she were still with Harley. How many black eyes, swollen lips and bruises would she have to suffer as the price for just existing? Did she really need Harley, or was it he that needed her?

The man beside her turned slightly. Mac moved over to the far edge of the bed, suddenly a little bit afraid of this stranger. What kind of man was he? He didn't drink. He didn't smoke. He hadn't even made a pass at her. Mac did not know men like him actually existed. He was a Christian, she supposed, but she did not know many Christians either. Was that what made him different? Was that really what made him offer to help her, or was it that he just needed to have someone around because he certainly was a lonely man. Mac remembered thinking that when she had served him at The Barn the night before. He came in alone. He sat alone. He ate alone. He didn't read anything. He seemed sad somehow, like he was an outcast from society. She had lingered by his table making small talk, smiling at him, trying to make him feel better, but then she did that with a lot of customers as she hustled for better tips.

Glancing at the clock radio on the lamp stand beside the bed, she wondered what Harley had done that night when he could not find her. Just thinking about how mad Harley would have been caused a knot to ball up in her stomach. If he had known where she was, at another man's house even though in a most innocent situation that was his fault, things would have been very unpleasant. A man as controlling as he had become was sure to cause trouble before the day was out.

Mac had learned to take not only each day as it came, but each hour, so while she feared the future, she just did not think too far ahead choosing instead to deal with Harley later. Maybe that was why she was still with him, always waiting until later to deal with him but so far, later had not come. There had been no good time or way to deal with someone like Harley without someone getting hurt. Right now she was in a clean bed, in a safe house, had had a wonderful supper and hot bath and had even managed to wash and dry her uniform. She would get through the day remembering how nice it had been. Mac was also very determined to grasp this opportunity to get out of the hell she had been living in and to do something more with her life. It was either that or let Harley beat her to death some night.

For now, however, she was someplace safe, warm, dry and away from Harley. She must have already died and gone to heaven.

Chapter Five
The Barn

"With emotional abuse, the insults, insinuations, criticism, and accusations slowly eat away at the victim's self-esteem until he or she is incapable of judging a situation realistically. He or she may begin to believe that there is something wrong with them or even fear they are losing their mind. They have become so beaten down emotionally that they blame themselves for the abuse." Beverly Engel

The Waffle Barn was the local hangout for the small, west Georgia community of Stonewall. It served breakfast 24/7/365. It never closed and boasted that there was not one minute in the past 10 years of operation that at least one customer wasn't being served. The record had reached the point that often a lone customer might linger over a cup of cold coffee until another customer arrived. The Waffle Barn was located in a remodeled, bright red barn that still had a roof with a sign 'See Rock City' painted on it. It was a real barn that still sat on what had been a real working farm, but the growing town had eventually moved out to and swallowed up the farm. The Barn featured tables in some of the old, original stalls and other tables stationed upstairs in the old loft. An elevator had been installed for access to them. The floors were wooden, stained and sticky with the everyday spilling of the imported maple syrup (all the way from Maine, they boasted). Some swore that the Waffle Barn smelled faintly of hay, but mostly the smell of burned bacon hung heavily in the air, along with the light aroma of freshly brewed coffee. It was the only thing in the place that seemed fresh to Mac except for the middle aged male customers who were constantly telling her dirty jokes and making obscene suggestions to her. There had been quite a scene one night when one overly frisky man actually pinched her. She turned around and slapped his false teeth right out of his mouth, watching them soar majestically across the room, knowing that she had just lost her job. The teeth hit two tables away and slid across the checkered table top before coming to rest in an elderly lady's surprised lap. It was then that Big Ed, the Waffle Barn owner, had come sailing out of his office and without asking a question, physically threw the man, and his teeth, out.

Big Ed was tough to work for, but he took care of his waitresses as if they were his own
daughters. He was 6' 6'' tall, thus the name "Big" Ed, and had played college football until his knees gave out. Now he spent twelve or fourteen hours a day in his little office adding up the sales receipts, filling out his weekly food orders, watching television, or sitting at the counter with some of his seemingly ever present cronies. This was the small group of men who hung out at The Barn drinking free coffee hour after hour and who were largely responsible for the boast that there had never been a moment without a customer in 10 years. Folks were careful not to use the term 'paying customers' when talking about them.

Big Ed left the cooking and over all running of the kitchen to Ella Mae (not Ellie Mae) but Ella Mae Johnson, a roundish, short black woman who had been with Ed since he opened. Everyone, even Ed, called her Momma because she was a mom to all the younger folks that worked there with her. She was a combination boss, mother, and father (or mother) confessor figure, quick to dispense her words of wisdom whether asked or not. Unknown to most, but not to Big Ed, was the help she had lent to some of the early leaders of the Civil Rights movement, allowing them to clandestinely meet in her home to plan marches or sit-ins while she comforted them with food and a safe place to rest. It was to her that Elizabeth MacIntosh reported the next morning for the early shift. Ella Mae, with apron on and scrambling eggs for the early morning truckers already assembled, called out to Elizabeth as she entered.

"You're early. For work. Somebody write that down on ta calendar that Mac made it in here not only on time, but early. Whatssa matter child? Hadn't you been home yet? I knows that Mista Harley haint' done been up and brought you to work. Come on, tell Momma all about it."

The young woman walked over to the bar in front of the grill where the black woman was working and talking. Mac plunked herself down on an empty stool and one of the other waitresses who was already on duty poured her a cup of coffee.

"Thanks, Meg. That looks wonderful." She sipped the hot, black coffee from her white cup that had a chip on the handle.

"Yo hadn't answered Momma. Yo even smilin. Yo must have had some night."

Elizabeth MacIntosh was afraid to answer, for if she verbalized her wonderful evening and the great opportunity she had been offered it might turn out to only have been a dream. She knew it was foolish to think that she could possibly live in that mansion with a total stranger, but he had been a perfect gentleman, even when she had given him the opportunity not to be.

Momma dished up three plates of bacon and runny, fried eggs and laid them on the counter for Meg to deliver to the three hungry truck drivers waiting patiently in the corner booth. Before she returned to her cooking, the rotund black woman put her hands on her hips and stared directly at Mac who was trying to avoid her gaze. "Now, Mac, I heard dat Harley was by here late yestedy aternoon to pick yo up, and he lefts heh in a huff when you wharnt' heh. I knows you didn't catch the bus home."

Mac was trapped and knew she had to give an answer, especially when she knew that Harley would be by later in the morning to bawl her out, and to get some beer money. Maybe if she gave him enough beer money he would leave her alone. "Well, Momma, I met this guy."

Meg hollered and Momma just grunted. "Go on, child, we're listenin."

"Well, I met him here and he offered to take me home so I let him and then when I didn't want to go into my roach motel of a trailer, he offered to let me use his daughter's room because she is moving out to live with his wife who just divorced him and he's lonely and needs someone to help him keep the house and he offered to bring me to work and pick me up and even to help me get a driver's license and he said I can stay there rent free and all I have to do is help keep the house straight." She rattled it all off without taking a breath. Silence fell over the diner. Even the truckers were straining to hear and shaking their heads disapprovingly.

Momma was holding a long wooden stirring spoon and pointed it at Mac. "How many times we gotta tellya. That man coulda kilt yo and he may not ask for payment now, but I guarantee he'll want payment later and nots in money."

Mac didn't want to hear anymore and stood up. "Yeah, well maybe so, but its sure better than getting beat up by a drunken, stinkin Harley. And just maybe I would be willing to pay." With that she grabbed a wet rag and stomped off to clean tables.

Much later in the morning, a loud motorcycle was heard roaring into the parking lot. The Waffle Barn had two customers that were either late for breakfast or early for lunch. They were lingering over a cup of coffee until the next customer arrived. It was Harley as Mac knew it would be. He stormed in wearing the same dirty clothes he had been wearing the night before, long, greasy hair streaming down around his shoulders, his face still barely covered by his thin beard. He sat down at the counter. Meg eased up to wait on him, but he was in a nasty mood. "Where is she?" he snarled.

Tiny, red headed Meg, who looked like she could be blown away in any windstorm, ignored the comment. "So what'll it be today, Harley? Momma's got some fresh pancakes on."

Harley was looking around the room trying to see if Mac was there. "Where's Mac?" he asked, this time with less attitude as the thought of pancakes made his stomach growl.

"She's in the back, today. Now you want those pancakes or not?"

He was hungry, he had to admit. Mac had not come over after work from the little trailer he had helped her rent near his to cook his supper as she did on most evenings. He had made a fried baloney sandwich with lots of mustard to kill the taste of the month old baloney and he ate some pork'n beans right out of the can washing it down with a six pack. He would like to have had more, but he was out of money and Mac wasn't around to borrow from. "Did she say where she was last night?"

Meg was writing down his order. "You want black coffee with that? It might help sober you up."

"I hope I ain't paying extra for the sauce you servin," he muttered. "You can nail that trap of yours shut, but yeah, bring me a pot of coffee. And give me a side of bacon with those pancakes."

Meg beamed at him. "Sure thing, Sugar. It'll be right out."

He called out to her back as she walked away. "Tell Mac I'm here and want to see her before I go."

Twenty-five minutes later Harley was feeling much better than when he had arrived. Knowing he would be, and hoping the growing lunchtime crowd would keep him from making a scene, Mac came through the swinging doors and sat down on the stool beside him. "Where'd you go last night?" he asked without looking at her.

She answered carefully as she noticed Momma had now positioned herself at the stove not very far away. "It was raining and you weren't here, so I caught a ride."

"Where to?"

"Home." It was true enough.

"I didn't see you there and I must have checked 10 times." The thought of Harley constantly watching her trailer to see if she was home was mildly funny, but it disturbed her to think how much control Harley had over her.

"Well, maybe I turned out the lights and went to bed."

"Yeah, well, maybe. So how did you get to work?"

"What is this? Twenty questions? I ain't your wife for you to keep check of."

Harley was getting angry now, but fought to control it. "You just remember who got you that trailer and who keeps you living there. Without me, you'd a been throwed outta there a long time ago and would be livin in the woods or somewhere worse."

"Yeah, well maybe I got me a better situation now, one without rats and roaches." She was getting angry in her turn.

"Sure, you have. And I'm the King of Italy. You just be careful cause I better not find out you been messing around with nobody. I wouldn't like that. Now what time do you get off today?"

Momma swung around from the stove. "I'm taking her home today, yo majesty, so why don't yo go out and try to find a real job?

Somethin besides fixin junk motorcycles. And take a bath and gets a haircut while yo are at it. And shave dat nasty face. It looks like dirt."

Harley stood up with a guttural growl and was ready to reach across and grab the black woman when Big Ed walked out of his office where he had been keeping a careful ear on the conversation. "You leavin now, Harley? Don't forget to leave a tip. Meg gets really mad when she don't get tipped."

Knowing that he was no match for Big Ed, at least not without his snub nosed .38, the dirty young man dug deep into his pocket and pulled out his last quarter. "I was just goin. Those pancakes done made me sick. I think I gotta go throw up or something. I sure hope I make it out the door in time." With a wry smile he looked at Mac. "I need some money."

Big Ed eased his way around the counter. "I'm not paying her anymore to keep your belly full of beer. Momma was right. You go get your own real job and quit sponging off women. It's high time you grew up. I would suggest you join the army, but you ain't man enough. They wouldn't have you, not even for cannon fodder."

Harley turned to leave, but not before spitting a nasty wad on the floor. With that and without another word he strode from the building. Big Ed looked at Mac. "I know it's not your fault, honey, but we can't have him keep coming in here causing scenes like that. You need to do something about him."

Mac was almost in tears, fearing she was about to lose her job. "Like what?" she asked quietly.

"Like finding someplace else to stay and getting away from him." Big Ed did not usually dispense advice since Momma had such a vast store of it, so when Big Ed spoke the girls listened. He patted her on the shoulder and left her under the watchful eye of Momma.

"Girl, how does you find these men?" she asked. "Now you get yo self back to work and don't worry about Harley. Big Ed won't let him bother you here."

"That's great," thought the young waitress. "But what about the other sixteen hours of the day?"

Chapter Six
Nasty Beats Nice

"It did not happen suddenly all at once or I would have left. It started with manipulation, control, and verbal abuse. It was so gradual that I never saw it coming."
Adrienne Thames

Wallace Harris was a nice guy. Everyone said he was a nice guy. He imagined that is what would be put on his tombstone some day. "HE WAS A NICE GUY." He was so nice that he had invited a strange woman home with him because she was in trouble. She had even slept in his bed. He had gone farther and invited her to stay permanently with him in his house that she considered to be a mansion but his only ulterior motives were that it would keep him from being so lonely and it would give him someone to help him keep the house clean. As he thought about it he hoped this young woman would say "Yes" and decide to stay with him because he hoped that he could make a difference in her life, and somehow that was important to him. It gave him something to live for, something that gave his life value. That morning before letting her off at The Barn, he had given her his cell phone number and asked her to call him. When she did call just after noon, he was pleased.

"Mr. Harris," she began. "This is Elizabeth MacIntosh." As if he could possibly forget that voice. "I've thought about your offer, and if it still stands, then I would love to try it."

Wallace was thrilled. "Great. Really great! And now please call me Wallace. Okay? And would you like me to pick you up after work?"

"Well, Wallace" she said. "Momma, that's our cook here who kind of takes care of us girls, has offered to take me by the trailer and get my things, not that I have much. She'll drop me off at your place. As much as she distrusts your motives, she hates Harley more. I think she wants to check you out, too. So what time will you get home?"

"Usually I get home by 5:30, but I can get off earlier if I need."

"Oh, no," she returned quickly. "We'll have to work all that kind of stuff out, but for now, I'll get Momma to bring me over at 6:00. That will give her plenty of time to sniff around and figure out if you intend to molest me or not."

Wallace laughed. He was actually beaming, though blushing. "I look forward to meeting her. I hope I can convince her that all I want to do is help and that in the process you can help me. We'll talk all about it tonight. See you then."

Mac hung up the phone and smiled to herself. "That Wallace sure is a nice guy," she thought. "And I'm going to do my best to help take care of him. If I could just figure a way to get Harley off my back."

Later that evening, Momma had met Wallace, snooped around his house and asked lots of questions.

"Where you from?" she asked as he showed them the house.

"I'm a native," he said. "Born and raised around Stonewall."

"How many kids ya got?"

"Just Lauren, my daughter, who starts college in the fall. She will be moving onto campus then."

"You must be about 40 then" They had toured Mac's bedroom which Momma found too close to his. "Why did you get divorced?"

Mac finally cut her off. "Momma! That's getting a little too personal."

"So is this heh strange man wantin you to live with him when ya don't really knows him."

Wallace shook his head at Mac. "It's okay. There are lots of reasons people get divorced. Rachel Lynn left me because she found somebody with a bigger car." They all laughed.

Momma looked at Wallace, then looked at Mac. "Yo not kiddin Momma are ya?"

Wallace shook his head. "I wish I were. All I can afford is that beat up sedan I drive."

"Like I told him," chimed in Mac. "It looks like a Cadillac to me."

Finally feeling satisfied that Wallace Harris had honest intentions, but somewhat distrustful because "he was still a man", Momma left. Wallace sat down in his living room with the young woman he was intent on rescuing. They talked about many things, about her responsibilities, about his desire to get her on her feet by helping get a driver's license and helping her get credit established. As they sat there, Mac looked at her rescuer and much to her surprise she found him cute in an odd sort of way. She liked the way he laughed and how his whole body shook when he did. His eyes would wrinkle up, he would grin big and the laugh would come from way down deep. Somehow, she realized that Wallace hadn't laughed much in a long time. "Maybe he will have the chance to laugh more with me helping him out," she thought. "Hopefully we can help each other get through a tough spot."

That evening as Wallace once again lay in bed watching an old movie, there was a knock at his door. Once again a sleepy, somewhat shy Elizabeth entered. Once again, with his permission, she lay down on her back beside him and they talked for a few minutes. Again he was a gentleman and did try to touch her or force his attentions on her. Before long, she dozed off, feeling safe, secure and not worried about rats, roaches, paying the rent or about having to 'pay' Wallace.

When her breathing became heavy, Wallace looked over at her. Was he seeing her as a daughter or was there some other possibility? No, he would not give his heart away again. It would kill him. Yet, he had known her a little more than twenty four hours and already she had brought her few meager possessions and moved in. She owned no furniture, nor much of anything besides a few clothes none of which were very nice. What jewelry she had owned, Harley had pawned long ago to support a growing alcohol addiction. Basically, she had nothing. As she lay there, he pitied anyone that could be in that position. He wondered how many times Mac had been beaten by Harley, bad enough to need a doctor, but had not gone because she could not afford it? He wondered how a person could live without health insurance, though he realized that many people did because they had to. Personally, he not only had health insurance at work, but a good life insurance policy that would pay out over a quarter of a million dollars if he died. Rachel Lynn had been his beneficiary, but he was now in the process of changing it. Who should get it? He supposed he would leave it to his daughter but with her in danger of becoming just like her mother, he wasn't so sure. Not that he intended to die anytime soon, but one needed to be prepared for such an eventuality. It was something Wallace was praying about and needed to resolve.

And what about this Harley character? Wallace wasn't sure but from the haunted look on Elizabeth's face, he could tell what little self-esteem she may have had at one time had been destroyed by Harley, likely by too many verbal attacks, scathing criticisms and demeaning remarks. Wallace himself had been victimized too often by Rachel Lynn's acerbic tongue and could only begin to imagine what Elizabeth had heard from Harley. Something would have to be done about him or Mac would have to quit The Barn and find a job where Harley would never find her. The Reverend Lee would know what to do. His son was a county deputy and would be able to offer sound advice. Yawning, Wallace turned the television off, determined to call the reverend in the morning.

Nailed

Earlier that afternoon, a motorcycle engine roared to life, sputtered, billowed out a dark gray cloud and died. Harley, who was known to his small group of co-workers and friends to be anything but nice, cursed as he knelt beside it. Before the smoke had cleared the garage, Harley had swilled another mouthful of some cheap beer that he hated. Now that Mac had disappeared from his life, he couldn't afford his usual beer and that made him mad. He wiped his mouth with the greasy back of his hand, mad that he couldn't get this motorcycle running after working on it for two days. He was mad that he had been forced to work extra to make up for his lost income and he was mad at Mac for running out on him when he had been so good to her. Hadn't he fixed it up with the owner of the trailer park to rent her that little unused, condemned by the county, trailer to her? Harley got half of that every month, a fact that Mac did not know. All she knew was that he had arranged it with a friend for her to live there. Now that income was gone, too.

Harley made several more adjustments. The engine roared to life and stayed. With a wide grin on his face he said to anyone who might have been listening over the roar of the machine, "I nailed it this time. It took some doing, but there ain't a bike made that I can't fix eventually." Satisfied that he had finally finished the job, Harley hopped on it and roared up and down the street in front of the motorcycle shop. It died on the far end of the street and would not crank again. Fifteen minutes later a tired, hot, sweating, cursing Harley pushed the cycle up in front of the shop and let it drop. Storming inside, he hollered for his boss.

"Jack!" he called with an obscenity. "I quit. You can fix this thing. I've had it." Jack, an overweight, middle-aged hippie who still wore his tie-died T-Shirts, had heard it all before. Harley quit two or three times a month, but would always come back sobered up and asking for work again. Jack went out and pushed the cycle back into the garage where someone else would work on it later. Harley was an excellent, almost gifted mechanic some said and could fix anything, but if he was having troubles at home as he often did, then he wasn't worth much.

Harley Martin was not a difficult man to understand. A battered son of an alcoholic father, he had once been married but his wife had left in the middle of the night. While he was passed out drunk, she had taken Harley's battered son with her and escaped. He never heard from them again and never tried to find them. A high school dropout, he never held a job long and lived only for the next beer. He had a long line of ex-girl friends, some that had stayed with him for several years until his verbal lashing and physical beatings of them got too hard to take. Mac had been with him over two years and he was very comfortable having her around. She cooked for him, did his wash, cleaned his trailer, and filled his 'other' needs. Now as he sped through the streets heading for his favorite liquor store his anger was directed not only at Mac but also at the man who had stolen her away from him. Some kind of business man. A sugar daddy. Nobody did that to Harley. Nobody.

Hours later he was working on the last of a six pack as he sat in his favorite chair, pointing his .38 Saturday Night Special at anything that moved on the old TV screen. He imagined that the actresses were Mac and the actors some invisible boyfriend of hers. She was trash. Who was she to move out of the trailer and beyond his control anyway? She was sorry, white, trailer trash and that is all she would ever be. He might not be able to get to her at The Barn and whip her, but he would catch up with her somewhere. Somehow, he would find out who the hotshot was she was staying with and he would deal with him, too. As he finally slipped into his usual beer induced coma, the sweetness of his ultimate revenge brought a smile to his face. The new boyfriend might be nice, but Harley could be nasty and nasty beat nice every time.

Chapter Seven
An Old Problem

"Looking back, I believe the verbal and emotional abuse was worse than the physical. With the physical, the wounds start to heal immediately. The emotional wounds last far beyond that and the emotional scars last forever. Whoever said sticks and stones may break my bones, but words could never hurt me has never experienced domestic violence and abuse. If they had, they would know the pain and destruction words can cause." **Adrienne Thames**

"You mash this button, and click here." Wallace leaned over a bewildered Elizabeth as he was showing her how to use the internet, specifically how to find the driver's license test. He was surprised at how little Elizabeth knew about operating a computer and "surfing the net". The internet was an unexplored universe for her since she did not yet have a mobile phone with access. The Department of Transportation website came up and Wallace let Mac look over it. She found a box that said "Written Exam" and clicked on it causing Wallace to smile to himself. She would learn quickly. After printing off a sample test, Wallace left Mac to explore this strange new world. Several times she called him and asked questions or was confused, but mostly she was able to navigate easily. She even did a search and found the website for the Waffle Barn, a site that Big Ed has recently launched with the help of the local high school computer classes. Later, the young woman sat at the kitchen table working on the sample test surprising herself but not a proud Wallace, as she used her common sense to make a 100 percent.

The next afternoon found Wallace standing beside Mac in line at the Driver's License Bureau, and before the afternoon was over, a smiling Mac climbed back into the passenger seat of the sedan. "What are you doing?" asked Wallace. "You have a license now. You drive me home."

"I can drive you know. I've done it before. I just never done it legal."

She drove home and except for one or two suggestions, Wallace did not make a comment about her driving. He remembered how terribly his daughter, Lauren, had driven the first time, in fact the first hundred times. She was still a terrible driver. At least now she would be on her mother's insurance and not his. It was obvious to Wallace that some people were just not ready for a license at age sixteen. At age twenty six, Elizabeth MacIntosh was ready.

As they wheeled into the subdivision, Wallace praised her ability. Turning into the driveway, she cheerfully remarked "We're home."

The remark seemed odd to Mac at first, that she should call this place home. She had met this strange man only days ago, was already was living in his home, sleeping in his bed at times, and driving his car. They had no physical relationship, and as far as she could tell, he did not desire one.

As they walked up the front steps, Mac turned suddenly to Wallace and took his hands in hers and stepping up on her toes, kissed him quickly on the cheek. An embarrassed and now red-faced Wallace put his amazed hand to the still wet spot on his cheek. "What is that all about?" he asked with a quizzical look on his face.

Mac ran up the steps and called back over her shoulder "That's for being such a nice guy. You're my hero." With that she ran lightly inside, still laughing at the strange look on Wallace's face. For the first time, the thought of actually being in love with someone flashed across her mind. Could she love this strange, lonely man and was she falling in love with him, or was it just a natural response to his rescuing her? Hurrying into what she now called "Her room", she closed the door and sat on the bed. What was love anyway? She had never loved Harley, she knew that.

58

Their relationship had been one of convenience for both of them, or so she had thought at first. On contemplating it further she realized that while it was been convenient for Harley, it was a desperate necessity for her survival, or had been until Wallace had come along. Sure Wallace was older than her, but she was long past caring what other people thought about her relationships. After being with Harley for so long and tolerating his abuse, she had very little pride left. Yes, she could love Wallace but could he love her? Harley had certainly made every effort to hammer into her how worthless she was and undeserving of anyone's love.

Later that evening as they cleaned up the supper dishes, Wallace asked Mac when she would be comfortable driving herself to work. When she asked about insurance, Wallace had simply said, "The car is insured, not you. We don't have to worry about that as long as the car is in my name. I'll call my agent tomorrow just to make sure."

"But what will you drive if I drive the sedan?"

Wallace had already figured that out. "Remember? My dad has an old truck that he is giving me."

"Have you told him about me?" So far, Mac had not been introduced into Wallace's world and knew very little about his family or even his background.

"Yes, I have talked to both Dad and Mom and they are anxious to meet you."

She was curious now as she washed off the plates. "And what did you tell them about our relationship?"

Wallace shrugged. "I just told them the truth. That I had met a young woman in trouble and was helping you out. I told them I wanted to let you drive my car and Dad said to take his truck because he wasn't driving it much anymore."

Mac turned the water off and began drying the two glasses. "Don't they think it weird that I live with you? Won't they think that we are, well, you know."

"Some things are just none of their business and they have too much decency to ask. Now back to my question. When do you want to start driving to work?"

She took a deep breath as the old, familiar knot of fear grabbed her insides. "Well, there's a problem that I need to tell you about."

"Harley Martin?" Wallace's answer surprised her.

"Yeah. How'd you know?" She had dreaded the moment when she would have to tell him about her fear of Harley and his threats.

"I'm a good customer at The Barn, remember? I hear things and I ask questions, too."

Mac felt herself getting mad. Turning on him she put her hands on her hips. "You've been checking up on me behind my back? Who have you been talking to? Momma?"

Wallace had not yet experienced her in this mood, but was ready to face the situation directly, something he had failed to do many times with Rachel Lynn. Maybe he had been too afraid of losing her. "Yes, I have talked to Momma, to Big Ed, and to several of your friends. Just like Momma checked me out, I've been checking you out. I know pretty much everything that they do about you. And I know that Harley is going to be a problem. You don't just walk away from guys like that without trouble."

Mac was almost out of control. "What gives you the right to go sneaking around behind my back and rooting into my personal affairs? You think just because you helped me out that you are entitled to treat me like some little girl? I'm not your daughter."

Wallace was sitting at the kitchen table. "Nor are you my wife. Yet you live in my house and have been sleeping in my bed, both of which made me extremely uncomfortable at first, but which I have come to accept. We need each other. You know that. And I'm ready to do whatever it takes to help you even if it means dealing with a drunken fool like Harley, but I needed to know some things about you, so I asked. And since I asked, I found out that Harley has been trying to follow us when we leave The Barn. Momma told me that."

This revelation hit the young woman like a punch in the belly from Harley and she collapsed into a chair beside Wallace. "He's trying to find out where I'm living?"

"Yes."

"Oh, no. What do we do? I can't leave town. I don't have anywhere else to go. All I can do is go back to him. If I don't someone will get hurt and I ain't gonna let that happen."

It was now Wallace's turn to reach out and take her hands tenderly in his as he looked deeply into her eyes of fear. "I know I'm not much to look at, but I think I can take care of Harley."

With a gut wrenching honesty, Mac replied, "He would chew you up and spit you out. He's mean, and you're not. He has no scruples. You do. If he finds us together, he will kill us both."

Reaching up, Wallace wiped a tear from the corner of her eye. Mac was ashamed because she saw crying as weakness. The weak do not survive, at least not in the world she had lived in. "You are right, Mac. If I tried to fight him, from what I have found out about him, he would literally stab me in the back without a second thought. Yeah, he's meaner than me, but give me some credit because I am smarter than him and will use that to my advantage when the time comes."

"What do you mean? What can you do?"

"Elizabeth, you don't know very much about me. One thing you will find out is that when I commit to something, like I have committed to helping you, I give it 100%. I am stubborn, hardheaded and sometimes just plain dense. I have set my mind on getting you out of this mess. I've already called Reverend Lee."

"You know 'the Will of God?'" Mac knew him from The Barn and had been the target of more than one of his tableside sermons.

"Sure. He's my preacher. Did you know his son is a Deputy Sheriff?"

"I didn't know he had a son."

Wallace got up. Walking over to the sink he pulled out one of the newly washed glasses and ran some water into it from the faucet. After drinking it completely, he answered. "Yep. Tad Lee has been a deputy for a couple of years. Reverend Lee talked to Tad and Tad is going to pay a little visit to Harley to warn him."

Mac laughed. "That will just make him madder. You don't know Harley. I warn you not to underestimate him."

"It's just part of the plan. He will have been officially warned so that will make it easier to get a restraining order."

Mac laughed again. "You were right. You are dense. Harley doesn't care about the law or the deputies or any restraining order. If he wants me back, he will not stop no matter what it takes or what it costs him. If he can't have me, then he'll make sure no one else does either. And he doesn't care about going to prison because he's been there before."

Chapter Eight
Fine Sermon

Jesus said "You will always have the poor among you, but you will not always have me." **John 12:8 NIV.**

Reverend Will Lee was sitting in the big recliner in Wallace Harris' living room while the couple sat on the sofa facing him. They were worried. "So you think he followed you home last night?" The preacher had received the call around noon that Harley had been spotted in their neighborhood that morning. His son Tad had then been called. He immediately hurried over and patrolled several times around the area, but when there was no sign of Harley he had gone to answer another call.

Mac shivered. "I'm sure it was him. I heard his bike. He must have followed me when I got off at midnight. He knows where we are now. If I know him, he'll go home, get liquored up, and come back to get me, maybe even with his gun. We shouldn't be here."

Wallace now spoke. "Will, I want you to take Elizabeth and go somewhere safe. I'll wait here until Harley comes, then call 9-1-1. Tad will get here before anything happens."

Their conversation was interrupted by a hammering on the door and cursing. The hammering stopped and kicking began. Mac jumped up in alarm, but Wallace sat frozen to his seat.

Quickly taking out his cell phone, the minister pushed a button. A moment later a voice said "Go ahead, Dad."

"Hey, Bub," Reverend Lee answered calmly as if nothing were happening. "Mr. Harley Martin has decided to pay a visit on Wallace Harris and Elizabeth. I'm still out here with them now and Mr. Harley is causing a big ruckus out front. I sure hope he doesn't tear that door down he's pounding on. He might find out what the Will of God is all about."

"On my way, but its going to take about 10 minutes to get there. Do I need a back-up?"

"No, Son," Reverend Lee grinned and Tad could feel it on his end. "You can come cover my back this time."

"Dad," replied the Deputy sharply. "Don't go doing something foolish. Just hold the fort until I get there, out."

Putting the phone down, the minister turned to Wallace. "Take the little lady here to the back bedroom and lock the door."

The cursing and hollering outside had intensified. Rocks were now being hurled against the house and the door. "What are you going to do?" asked a horrified Elizabeth. "He's drunk and he's going to hurt somebody and it won't be the first time. He's going to swing at anybody in sight. Maybe I should go out and talk to him." She started moving towards the door.

Wallace, admiring her courage or foolishness, grabbed her. Holding up his Bible, Will of God declared almost as a prophet of old might "I'll handle it. I am going to hit him with some words from the Good Book. Now y'all go on back and lock yourselves in and don't come out until I say." He pushed them from the room and turning, went out the back sliding glass door. Easing around the edge of the house, he peeked towards the front porch and saw Harley going back up the steps. Will did not see a weapon.

Acting like he was making a planned visit, the Will of God walked up the steps, Bible in hand. "Hey, friend," he called cordially with a smile. "What's all the fuss about, Son?"

64

Seeing the Bible, a sullen and obviously drunken Harley snarled "You get out from here, mister. This ain't none of your business and I ain't yor son."

William Lee continued walking up the steps, the smile still on his face. "You're wrong there, friend. These are my church members and you are bothering them. I'd advise you to go home and sleep it off."

Harley turned towards the preacher, fists clenched. "I said this ain't yor business, preacher man. Unless you want some of me, you'd better go bother somebody else with your good book."

The preached stopped just a foot away. Harley did not back up. He reeked of beer and old sweat. The preacher hated the well-remembered smell. "What you need, fellow, is a dose of the Good Book. In Matthew in the sermon on the mount….."

"You ain't preaching to me!" With that the drunken man hurled a fist at the preacher's nose. Expecting the action, William Lee stepped deftly to one side and the blow whistled by his left ear. Grabbing the extended arm with his right hand, the minister quickly twisted it around and stepped behind Harley, pulling the arm behind his back, almost to the younger man's neck. Harley screamed in pain until the Bible in the preacher's left hand came up viciously against his wind pipe, effectively choking off Harley's breath and scream.

"Now, you listen to me," the preacher said in a low forceful voice in Harley's ear, a voice that not even his congregation had ever heard on his hardest sermon, a voice he had not used for many years. "My name is Reverend Will Lee of the First Christian Church of Stonewall. People call me 'The Will of God.' He eased his grip on Harley's throat just a bit. When Harley began to thrash around and try to kick him he pushed his Bible back into the struggling man's Adam's apple again. "Today you can call me 'The Right Hand of the Almighty God.'" Applying even more pressure he continued. "Vengeance is mine, I will repay, saith the Lord". Harley continued to thrash.

"Today," said the Reverend Lee with even more force, "I am the Lord's vengeance on you." He pushed Harley's arm up even higher eliciting a terrible moan of pain as a siren was howling in the distance. "Here's what's going to happen, Son. I am going to drive you home where you will sleep this off. Tomorrow is Sunday, so the first thing tomorrow morning you will present yourself sober, clean and freshly shaved, to me at church. If you are not there, two of the meanest, ugliest deacons you have ever seen, and their equally mean wives, will come and visit you and they will continue to visit you each and every day until you come to church."

Totally defeated and needing air, the young man slumped against Will Lee. Again relaxing his grip against the windpipe, the preacher eased the man's arm down. Realizing that the fight had been taken out of him, Will released him completely as the screaming siren of his son, Tad, whirled up the driveway. A young man as tall and burly as Will stepped out, there being little doubt as to who his father was. He was fair-haired and had a deep dimple in his chin.

Looking up at his dad, Officer Tad Lee called out "I thought I told you to wait until I got here."

"Well," his father said, now smiling again. "Harley here didn't get that memo and had other ideas. He just couldn't wait for you to arrive, so he and I had a little prayer meeting right here on the front porch. It was great. I told him all about the will of God. Now all Harley wants to do is go home and sleep it off. And tomorrow he's going to clean himself up and come to church. Aren't you boy?" He nudged the younger man in the back with his Bible.

"Yes sir," he mumbled. "I'll be there."

"Good!" The preacher was very happy. "Since my son is here, why don't we let him drive you home and I will follow him in your old truck."

Pulling out his cell phone, he dialed Wallace's number. "Hey, Wallace!" he called into the phone. "You can come out now. Tad's here and we are going to take this poor, old fellow home. Seems like he's had an asthma attack or something and is having a hard time breathing. His shoulder is really aching, too. Y'all just wait until we're gone before you come out. Oh, and Harley has promised to come to church tomorrow. I don't expect he will make it to the early service, so why don't you and Elizabeth come to it just so you can avoid him for a while. Great….see you then."

A few minutes later, the Reverend William Lee and son, Tad, were escorting a very tired, sobering, pained Harley Martin through the door of his trailer. A young woman looked up as they entered. She was wearing a Waffle Barn uniform and smelled lightly of smoky bacon.

"Wanda!" called the preacher. "What are you doing here?"

"I've been living here for a while. I needed a place to stay after my husband kicked me out. What's my drunk of a brother done this time?"

William Lee turned around to his son. "I can take it from here. Thanks for your help and call me when you get off work. I got some steaks we can grill out."

The big police officer nodded and left the room. Turning back to the waitress, the minister said "Harley promised to come to church tomorrow. Why don't you come with him? The service starts at 11:00 am."

Harley had already stumbled into his bedroom and closed the door. "Harley wants to go to church? Since when? You can't get saved when you're bombed out of your gourd can you?"

The preacher smiled. "Oh, I had to twist his arm a little bit, but I think he wants to be there. I threatened to send some deacons and their wives after him. Now, how about you? Every Saturday when I see you at The Barn you promise you'll come to church."

"I work a lot, Preacher, so you good Christians can come by before, after or when you're playing hooky from church. Somebody has to work to serve all of y'all. Besides, what good is going to church with all those hypocrites going to do me and Harley? I haven't exactly seen you over here trying to help folks that need it. That is what being a Christian is all about isn't, helping folks?"

Reverend Lee considered her statement. "Yes, Wanda. Helping each other is much of what being a Christian is."

The waitress sat down on the worn sofa to rub her tired feet. "How many of these folks living over here in Happy Valley have you helped? I drive by that big, fancy church of yours and think how much good that monthly payment on that monstrosity would do out here. You could change lives, give people some decent places to live. You might could even help deadbeat drunks like my sorry brother get some help. But most of you Christians don't want drunks and drug addicts coming to your church. You might send a little money but you certainly don't want to go get your hands dirty by getting involved in our messy lives. Jesus might condescend to men of low estate and eat with us humble sinners but most Christians don't want to be bothered."

The reverend suddenly found himself defending a position that he was very uncomfortable defending. "We do send 15% of our monthly income to missions. We have a really strong mission program."

"Mission programs," snorted the critical young woman. "That's not helping me pay bills. You think I like living in the middle of all this mess? How much do you make a year? $50,000? $60,000? 6 figures maybe? You live in a nice, big, comfortable house, too, don't you? Quiet neighborhood probably. You should come over here some Friday night. There's no peace and quiet out here then. We got some folks living out here that get real rowdy on the weekends, my brother

68

included. I'm sure your son can tell you some tales about the folks that get arrested out here every weekend. The TV show 'COPS' could make a whole series just filming some of these folks. Some are just drunks, but others have gotten into crystal meth. That stuff will mess you up. Yet, most of us out here are quiet, respectable, law abiding citizens who are just struggling to make ends meet like most folks in your church. It's the bad ones living out here that makes folks stereotype the rest of us. A few bad seeds make us all look bad, but all we want is to live comfortably like anyone else. But your good church members see me living out here and automatically think 'trailer trash'. So they keep their distance, and when it comes time to tip me at The Barn, the change comes out and the currency stays in the wallet."

"The church can only do so much." Reverend Lee found there wasn't much he could say now.

The waitress continued. "I bet you church people don't even know we have homeless people living in the woods in our little community. Has your son ever told you about them?"

The man had to admit that he did not know. "I guess I don't get out much from my congregation, Wanda. If we knew where any homeless were we would do what we could to get them into a shelter somewhere."

"Is that right? Well, I'll be sure to tell Herbert to look you up the next times he staggers into The Barn to get out of the cold, the rain, or to use the john. He lives in a tent across the road behind the liquor store. Very convenient. When he's not drinking some cheap whiskey, he's swilling down mouthwash. He's not doing that to kill bad breath either. But that's okay because the rest of him stinks so bad that you never smell his breath anyway. Imagine the stir it would cause if he showed up like that at your fancy church some Sunday morning. Your precious deacons would probably not even let him in. I don't know how many times one of us waitresses has taken some of our money from the tip jar to pay for him a meal."

"I'm sorry," was all the guilty minister could say. "I didn't know."

"Well, now you do. You go back to those church folks of yours and do something about it. We get these so called 'Social Justice Warriors' that come round here only at election time yacking about voting for them or their political party to end injustice to us by giving us more government aid. Oh, they are so concerned and want to help. Then they disappear until the next election and that promised help never arrives. We don't want more of their type of government in our lives. We're just like you and want access to the same opportunities you have, that's all. Help us get up on our feet and we'll take it from there. Help us help ourselves, that's all we ask."

Will of God realized that this was the finest sermon he had ever heard preached, better than any he had ever managed to deliver from his pulpit. The thing about a good sermon was that it helped one see where they were failing and inspired them to do better. He was already repenting of his failure to help meet the needs of these people "At least I'm here today," he answered. "I've never been here before, but I promise it won't be the last time I'm out here. If we do anything to help, it's going to take some input and direction from people like you that know where the real need is." He was already thinking about the help he could call in from local merchants who were in debt to him. Repentance required action he had preached to his congregation, and he was repenting now of his inaction.

"I would like to help you with that, Reverend Will. I really would." She was moved by the Will of God's concern.

"So, are you working tomorrow? I'd like to introduce you to some of the folks at church. Not the hypocrites though. Just the good folks."

Wanda laughed. "Okay. I'll be there and you can count on my getting Harley there, too. At least this once. But don't be surprised if he sleeps through the service."

The minister shook her hand. "You do that. And you remind him that he is supposed to shave, too." As Will Lee drove out of the trailer park that day, he determined to come back. Soon. He also planned to ask his son to help him find Herbert. "There's a lot of work to be done out here," he thought. "There's a lot of plowing to do in people's hearts, but you can't minister to the spiritual until you've relieved the misery of the physical. Lord, give me the wisdom and the strength and the means to bring Jesus to these folks."

Chapter Nine
Shopping Spree

"The heart will break, but broken live on." Lord Byron

Lauren could not believe what her father was telling her. She had expected it from her mother, but now her father was shacked up with some cheap, young thing? Talk about a mid-life crisis.

Wallace gripped the phone tightly as he continued his story, trying to ignore his daughter's sounds of dismay. "Her name is Elizabeth MacIntosh. She will be staying with me as long as she likes."

His teenage daughter wanted to hang up. Or throw up. Her parent's divorce had rocked her world, a blow from which she still had not recovered. Living with her mother and Roger had not been the heaven her mother had promised her it would be. She spent most of her time alone, at home, as her mother and her new husband spent a lot of time traveling for his job. Now she could not go home again as there was a new woman there that she never intended to meet.

"Lauren, I need your help. Elizabeth basically has no clothes besides her uniform and a few worn out T-shirts. I've never been good at shopping for women, you know that yourself. I quit buying for you and your mother years ago when you started returning everything I bought."

The girl snorted. "Daddy, really. We did that out of spite. This Elizabeth is a woman. Give her your credit card and turn her loose at the mall. It's instinct. She'll get herself a new wardrobe at your expense and then be off looking for a new boyfriend."

Wallace was in no mood to plead. "You don't understand. She has never had enough money to even go to the mall before. She has never shopped. She knows nothing about it. What rags she has have been given to her. From Goodwill or the Red Cross. Now can I count on you or not?"

Lauren hated these guilt trips. Life with her parents had been one guilt trip after another. Hearing them arguing seemingly night after night, for some reason, she thought the arguments were about her, for years blaming herself for their troubles. The only good thing about the divorce was that her parents tried to cover their own guilt by buying her things. Wallace couldn't afford a lot, but he did still give her a weekly allowance. "Does it have to be this afternoon?" she whined, much like her mother. If she had inherited anything from her father, it was that soft spot in the heart which her father had now touched.

"It really does. I want to take Elizabeth to church tomorrow but she says she can't go because she doesn't have anything to wear. Can we come pick you up?"

"Well......"

"I'll give you a $200 limit plus dinner at the Mexican place you like."

It was beginning to sound like fun. "Well, okay. But I'll meet you at the mall at the food court entrance."

After hanging up, Wallace knew he still had one more battle to fight. He found Elizabeth curled up in a fetal tuck on the sofa, still letting the shock of Harley's visit earlier in the day wear off.

He sat down in the big chair across from her. "Mac, I've got a surprise for you."

There was no response. "I've just talked with my daughter and she wants to meet you."

Still no response. "I told her we would meet her at the mall in 20 minutes."

The young woman, determined not to give in, sat up. "Listen, Wallace. I don't really feel like it. Not today."

"Sure you do. After that Harley mess we need to get away from here for a little while. We're going shopping, going to eat some Mexican food, and maybe take in a movie."

Elizabeth "Mac" MacIntosh could not comprehend what he was offering. She had never been shopping, had never eaten at a Mexican restaurant, and hadn't been to a movie in over 10 years. "Is this a date or something?" She looked at him warily.

"No!" the now stricken man responded quickly. "Nothing like that. I want you to meet Lauren and she is going to help you shop for some clothes. You're going to church with me in the morning."

"Sorry, Charlie," she said standing up. "I'm working tomorrow afternoon. Besides, I can't afford new clothes. And I don't do church. Too many Christians there."

"You can go to church just this once. We're going to the early service in the morning. I'm buying your clothes this evening so you will have something to wear. You can pay me back later if you want to. Now come on. It'll be fun. Lauren has already agreed."

Feeling her face flush with emotion, she suddenly wanted to rush the man and kiss him passionately. She could not imagine why he had taken such an interest in her and how he managed to know just exactly where she needed help the most. She hoped fervently that she was not falling in love with him, knight in shining armor to her though he was. Wasn't he old enough to be her father, as he had told her on several occasions? And wasn't he still in love with his ex-wife? And what would the girls, and Momma, at The Barn be saying already? Harley, too, was still to be reckoned with and that was a scary thought. Fighting back her impulse she finally laughed. "Okay, Sir Galahad. Let's mount your trusty steed and ride out to fight this dragon. But I'm still not sure about that church thing. God ain't never done too much for me and it's too late for him to start now."

After the phone call, Lauren Harris had quickly brushed her hair before dashing out to her car. Lauren was a normal teenage girl. She was just shorter than her father, definitely had his eyes and nose, and up until recently would not have been caught dead with him in the mall. Lately, she had noticed that she had begun to cherish their too brief hours together, even if they were hours where they might be spotted in public by her friends. As she paced along the curb waiting for them, she realized that she was somewhat jealous that her father was spending his time, attention and money on someone else. Secretly she had hoped that her mother and Roger would break up and then her parents could get back together, though deep down she knew that would never happen. Wearing her hair long and loose over her shoulders, she had on a beautiful maroon pull-over top that her mother had given her and the most expensive jeans she had been able to find. Her tennis shoes alone cost over $100. A gold necklace given to her by Roger completed her ensemble.

She saw the embarrassing sedan pulling into the lot and wondered how any self-respecting woman could be caught dead in it. She certainly hadn't wanted her friends at the mall to see her getting out of it. Watching anxiously, she watched as her dad parked the car at the far end of the lot as he always did. She wondered if he was ashamed to be seen in it or maybe if he felt it wasn't worthy enough to park alongside nicer vehicles. Watching as a young woman got out of the passenger side, Lauren, who had almost expected the woman to get out wearing a burlap bag, was suddenly self-conscious of how she was dressed. She had intentionally dressed in her best outfit just to impress this woman, but this woman who was approaching her now looked, well, she looked poor. She wore a jersey that was too large and jeans that obviously had seen other owners. Her hair was short, but clean and combed and she wore no makeup. There was nothing, absolutely nothing, attractive about her. In that moment her heart went out to the young woman. She might not be attractive at this moment, but she would be a knock-out before this evening was over.

Her dad was smiling, something she hadn't seen him do in a long time. He hugged his daughter and commented on how nice she looked. She wished he had not mentioned it. "And this," he said turning to the other young woman, "is Elizabeth MacIntosh. Elizabeth, this is my daughter Lauren."

It was a hard moment for Mac. She instantly noted how nice this young woman looked. Very nice. Mac wondered if she could ever hope to look that way. The women shook hands, then Lauren surprised herself, her father and Elizabeth by stepping up and hugging her tightly. Lauren now understood why her father had taken this girl under his wings and she determined to do the same. Mac was simply a woman that needed help. Nothing except a very extreme makeover would help her.

"Okay, Daddy," she said stepping back. "Give me your credit card and you go off and do whatever it is you men do while we women shop. Go down to Sears and stand in front of the TV section and see what's on. We girls are going to do the mall. But don't let the salesman sell you a television because our little shopping spree is already going to put you over budget for a long time to come."

Putting her arm through Elizabeth's she took command. "You just leave everything to me."

As Wallace watched them, he was once again amazed at Mac's inner beauty that had begun to reveal itself to him. The once harsh features on her face had begun to melt and merge into something softer that Wallace was glad to see. She was changing outwardly, too, not cursing as much or as freely, not as fearful of the dark, and more aware of how she looked when Wallace was around. She was like a butterfly struggling to get out of its cocoon, still there, but making an effort to show the world its real beauty. Wallace forced himself to fight what he realized was a growing attraction to her.

Two and a half hours later Wallace was sitting in the Mexican Restaurant waiting, when he saw two women approaching him, laughing and carrying large, full shopping bags. He barely recognized his daughter as her beautiful long hair was gone and a short, smart looking cut had taken its place. She stopped at his table, dropped her bags and put one hand on her hip and the other to her hair. "Well, Daddy, what do you think?"

Standing, Wallace was impressed. He had loved his daughter's long hair, but this was very nice, too. "We went into the Hair Salon and they were looking for long hair to cut to send to make wigs for girls with cancer, so I told them to whack away. Do you like it?"

Her father laughed and hugged her tightly. Neither one worried about the people who were staring at them or the waitress who stood by waiting for them to sit down.

Pushing back, Lauren now turned to the woman who had been hidden behind her. "And now may I present 'Elizabeth, shopper extraordinaire.'"

Wallace gaped at the transformation that had taken place. The blond hair now had a cute curl in it. Her fingernails were painted, as were Lauren's. She wore a button up the front print shirt with two pockets (with buttons) and a pair of tan slacks with comfortable looking brown loafers. Standing before him with a wry smile was not the poor looking woman of earlier in the day but a lovely young woman who was ready to meet her new world.

Not wanting to embarrass her, Wallace quickly motioned for them to sit down. As they did Lauren leaned over and whispered in his ear. "Don't worry, Dad. I didn't go over your limit, but Roger's card took a whooping today." For some reason, her father wanted to burst out laughing, but he just looked at his daughter with a newly found respect and mouthed "Thank you." Lauren understood that she and her father had just entered a new relationship that she could never hope to have with her mother.

During their dinner, Wallace found it hard to keep his eyes off the girls sitting across from him as he tried to adjust to their new looks. "Oh, Mom will kill me," Lauren said at one point about her hair. "But I will blame it all on you, Dad. Mom will understand that and hate you all the more." They all laughed. As he gazed at Mac, Wallace realized that the butterfly had emerged and was preparing to fly. That it might fly away scared him.

The evening had gone much better than Wallace could have ever expected, but it was the unexpected that troubled him. They had returned to the house and were walking up the front steps in the dark when it happened. Mac reached the top step first and turned around to thank him for the wonderful evening when she found herself not only eyeball to eyeball with him but nose to nose and lip to lip. They gazed at each other through the darkness for only a moment and before either one knew what was happening, they were kissing each other and enjoying it! They pulled away momentarily to question each other with their eyes, then kissed long and hard again. Suddenly, Wallace stopped, mumbled an apology and without further comment rushed into the house.

Later that evening after the movie, a tired, confused Wallace collapsed into his bed and as usual turned on his television to watch the news. As expected, there was a tap at his door and as expected, a shy Mac entered. She was wearing her worn out T-shirt and shorts again that she slept in every night, but her hair was still curled cutely to her head. She was not carrying her pillow.

Standing in front of him, Elizabeth knew she had to address the situation. "Wallace," she said, "it's alright. I liked the kiss. It was an impulsive thing that just happened. It was a very nice end to a very nice evening. I've never had an evening like it. Now I know how Cinderella must have felt. Don't let that kiss bother you. It's okay."

Wallace had been fighting with his emotions since that moment on the steps. He had never intended for that to happen and was terribly disappointed in himself for giving into that moment's weakness. "I'm sorry....," he began but she cut him off.

"Please, don't be. It was the right thing at the right moment. Believe that. It doesn't mean we have to get married or anything. " They both laughed then and the mood lightened, but they both realized that the kiss had moved their relationship into a new area. "I like you a lot, Wallace. I have to be honest with you. And not just because you are doing nice things for me. You are like no man I have ever met before. I didn't know men like you existed." There was an embarrassed silence before she went on. "Let's just leave it at that for now."

Wallace finally spoke. "Mac," he said slowly, looking into her eyes. "I've been hurt really bad by a woman that I still love deeply. I don't know that I can ever love again. Despite the fact that she is married, I felt like I betrayed her tonight when I kissed you. Besides that, I am way too old for you."

The young woman, fighting another urge to smother him in kisses, reluctantly kept a short distance between them.. "What happened tonight was a natural thing between two people who are hurting and finding comfort in each other. It was a kiss. Nothing more. Okay? So don't ruin it. I'm going to cherish it for a long time. Now you go to bed. I seem to remember that we are going to the early service at church in the morning."

As she left the room, Wallace fought off a rising feeling of panic as he realized that if unchecked, he would fall desperately and madly in love with this woman. He did not want to love again. Being in love hurt too much.

80

Chapter Ten
Attacked

"I was so scared of him at that point that I would not even fight back because I knew he would kill me. I could tell by the look in his eyes when he would wrap his hands around my neck that he was capable of it. He would watch the life start to leave my eyes as he choked me then let go so I could gasp for air. He would threaten that if I ever left him, he would hunt me down and finish me off for good."
Adrienne Thames

The voice of Reverend William Deveraux Lee boomed across the congregation. He spoke in his country drawl, but it sounded high, lofty, educated and straight from God to Elizabeth MacIntosh who had never heard the Reverend Lee preach before. It was as if God were speaking directly to her heart about God's love and God's desire for everyone to be saved. Elizabeth figured she had done too much wrong in her life for God to want to save her, from what she wasn't exactly sure, but it was nice to hear that at least God cared.

"For God loved the world, and that means each and every one of us, he gave his one and only son to die for us on that old, rugged cross." Reverend Lee made sure he made eye contact with Elizabeth as he said those words.

"Sure sounds nice," thought the young woman, "but ain't nobody ever cared enough about me to die for me. Why should God? I ain't worth it."

With the benediction concluded, the minister greeted the worshippers at the back door. He shook Wallace's hand vigorously and hugged Elizabeth who was still not used to all the authentic love and concern of Christian people. She could only remember being in church once or twice in her life and those occasions had been funerals.

"We'll see whether Harley shows up here in a little while," the minister beamed. "I think he will have sobered up by now. I took the liberty of removing all the alcohol from his trailer." He winked mischievously at Wallace.

"Then you had better watch the offering plate," replied a nervous Elizabeth, "because he will do anything to get his beer money. Ain't no store gonna be safe in this town until he gets it."

"Maybe he will get saved and won't want any after today," the minister answered, half seriously. "Everybody has potential in God's sight, and that includes Harley. He could be a changed man if he were to get his heart right with God."

"Then you had better pray that this building is built real good because the roof will fall in if he does." Elizabeth was not smiling as she spoke.

At that moment Harley Martin was standing in front of his refrigerator cursing the world loudly. "You ain't going to find no beer in there," said his sister, who entered the room wearing a nice dress and combing her hair. "The preacher threw it all out yesterday when he drug you home drunker'n Cooter Brown. He said you wouldn't make it to church sober if he left it here."

More cursing followed. "Church? Who said anything about going to church?"

His sister laughed. "You were so drunk yesterday you don't know what was going on. You promised to shave and clean up and be at church by 11:00. It's already 10:15, so you had better get moving."

"I ain't going to no church today nor any other day," snarled Harley.

Nailed

No sooner had the words left his mouth than there was a knock on the door. His sister opened it to see a deputy standing there. "Good morning, mam," he said, holding his hat in his hands. "I'm supposed to make sure that Mr. Harley Martin of this address gets himself to church today. It seems that if he don't, Reverend Lee will swear out a warrant for his arrest on assault and battery charges."

Harley pushed by his sister and looked down the steps at the deputy. "I ain't attacked nobody and I ain't going to church. Take that thesis and nail it to yor wall, Luther."

The smile left the deputy's face. He touched the walkie-talkie button on his shirt. "Yeah, Mr. Martin is resisting and refusing like we expected. I think we are going to need that warrant. Should I cuff him and bring him in?" Then the deputy's voice grew hard. "No I won't need back-up. I can handle him." He put his hand down on his holstered yellow and black stun gun as he said it.

The fight drained out of Harley. He knew that going to jail on Sunday morning meant being there until at least Monday afternoon. And he couldn't afford a lawyer or a fine. He didn't exactly remember what he had done or who he had attacked or why, but it must have been serious for this deputy to be here staring him in the face. "Oh, all right," he snapped. "I'll go, but I don't have to like it."

Right at 11:00 am as the band was entering the worship center and began singing, a freshly shaved Harley walked in the back door of the large church just behind his sister. Harley's hair was combed and he wore a nice, clean pair of jeans and a pressed, long sleeved white shirt. They sat as close to the back as possible. Throughout the service Harley rubbed his shoulder, not sure why it was hurting but assuming it had to do with his problems of the day before. Unfortunately, he did not hear the songs and missed the sermon completely, the same one the minister had preached at the first service. Harley missed the words about God loving him so much he had sent his son to die for him and he missed the preacher's glance in his direction as he said them. His mind had totally cleared from the alcohol induced fog of the day before, but as the sermon approached its conclusion, his thoughts were consumed with his growing hatred of Mac and the man she was living with. All Harley remembered from the day before was his determination to find Mac and bring her back where she belonged. He did not really love her, but she did owe him and he had taken good care of her when she needed it. Besides, without her, his beer money was seriously curtailed and he would have to work more hours. Less beer and more work was not appealing to the motorcycle mechanic. It would take time to find someone to replace her.

Just as Elizabeth and Wallace had done at the end of the early service, the crowd filed out greeting Reverend Lee as they left. Reverend Lee made sure to shake Harley's hand long and hard and pat him hard on the sore shoulder. "No hard feelings about yesterday, Harley."

Harley wondered again what had happened. "Did I do something wrong, sir?" Harley could be more than polite when required, if he was sober enough. Right now he was more sober than he enjoyed being.

"Well," replied the minister, "You were attacking the house where Elizabeth is living now, and when I intervened you threw a punch at me. It was all I could do to keep my deputy son from whipping you and throwing you in jail. I think you need to stay away from Elizabeth now."

Slowly Harley's memory of the event was returning along with his anger towards this preacher who had not only interfered in his affairs, but had thrown out all his beer. Realizing other people were waiting to greet the minister, Harley pushed by the big man but had a parting shot over his shoulder. "Don't preach me another sermon, Reverend. To get nailed with one boring sermon today is one too many. Maybe I will see you again real soon. Just don't expect it to be in church."

Nailed

The Will of God did not misunderstand the implied threat. It did not bother him because he had been threatened by bigger men that Harley. "Go with God, now or later," he prayed under his breath at the back of Harley Martin.

At that moment there was quite a stir among the employees of the Waffle Barn when Elizabeth arrived for her shift that Sunday. Her new haircut complete with the cute little curls had all the girls abuzz. Big Ed stormed out of his office to see what all the commotion was about and stopped in his tracks. "Girl," he said sincerely. "I would appreciate it very much if you would wear a hat and cover up that purdy new hairdo because if you don't, then I'm going to stay busy this evening throwing out all the guys who make passes at you while you stay busy knocking their teeth out."

Elizabeth giggled and blushed. Big Ed did not throw compliments like that around easily and in fact he had never complimented this young waitress on her looks. Standing over the stove stirring her 100th gallon of grits that day, Momma did not say a word, but did raise her eyes in wonder and happiness, happiness that one of her girls was having something wonderful happen to her.

Just before finishing her shift, Momma finally got the young lady by herself. "So, I hear you got some new clothes, too. And you met his daughter. Sounds like Mr. Harris done been thinkin about gettin real serious with you girl. Ya better watch yoself now and start locking your door at night, and if he kisses ya, ya get outta there."

One look at Elizabeth's little grin was all that the black matron needed. "Oh, my Lord, you dun kissed im. Tell Momma, now. You dun kissed im. I warned ya."

"Oh, Momma," the waitress retorted. "It was just a little good night kiss at his front door that just happened. It was an accident."

Momma grunted. "And you being conceived and standing here is an accident. Just listen to Momma and be careful." Another thought suddenly dawned on the woman. "Oh, Lordy. You fallin in love. I can see it in yo eyes and in yo face and in the way yo been carryin yo head tonight and in the way you walk. You in luv, child. Come on now, fess up to Momma. I knows it anyhow."

"Now Momma," protested the girl. "It was only a kiss that just happened. Why can't a man and a woman just be good friends without everybody thinking something's going on when it is really not. He's almost fifty years old. He's way too old for me."

Momma grunted. They had finished cleaning the counters, put on their coats and now were standing just outside the door waiting on Big Ed to walk them to their cars. "Yo remember. He's lonely. And a lonely man's a dangerous man. Tryin to buy yo affection. I've been roun the block a time or two. Yo mark my words." With that the black woman hugged her charge and hurried out to her car without Big Ed.

Looking back inside The Barn where one waitress would work through the night with one cook, Elizabeth saw the light in Ed's office still on. "He must be on the phone," thought a tired Elizabeth. Shrugging her shoulders she marched resolutely out to Wallace's sedan that she was now driving. In the shadows in front of the car she heard a scratching noise and saw a match flare. As it was raised to light a cigarette, a startled Elizabeth saw the rough, but clean shaven face, of Harley Martin.

Without a word he stepped over and before she could move he slapped her so hard across the face with the back of his hand that it knocked her to the ground. Standing over her he reached down and searched her pockets until he found her tip money, about $35. "You ready to come back home yet, Mac?" he asked with a sneer. She crawled to her knees and felt the blood trickling from the corner of her swiftly swelling eye. "You had better come back if you know what's good for ya. I heard about your little trip to the mall and your fancy new haircut. Don't start thinkin you're better than me, cause you ain't. You were born a nuthin, have always been a nuthin, and will always be a nuthin. You know what we are don't you? We're what they call "stereotypes", people who were born to a mold and have to stay there. We have to live up, or live down, to the expectations of the world. We can't change who we are or what we are. I was born to be a beer drinking, hell raising, best there's ever been motorcycle mechanic and you were born to keep guys like me happy. Don't go forgettin who you are or where you came from or what your place in this world is. We're from that mythical place they call 'the other side of the tracks', tracks they built and maintain, tracks to keep us in our place, except these tracks are imaginary ones that keeps them separated and away from us low lifes. You and me was born to this world of sorrow and we'll die together in this world of sorrow." He kicked out at her viciously, hitting her hard in the side with his boot. She collapsed onto her face again in tears. "Nuthin," he spat again. "You are a nuthin." Without another word, Harley turned and walked quickly away. Elizabeth heard him trying to start his motorcycle somewhere in the dark, and heard him curse when it would not fire immediately. It finally sputtered to life and after another moment or two Harley was roaring away into the night to visit his local beer store.

Crawling in terrible pain to the car, Elizabeth's one thought was to get away before Ed saw her. She knew what Ed would do. He would go find Harley and by the end of that meeting somebody would be dead. Elizabeth wiped the blood from her eye where it had trickled down into her mouth and managed to stand up. She opened the car door, noticing her right hand hurt terribly from where she had fallen on it. Almost sick to her stomach from the pain in her face, arm and side, she managed to get the car cranked. It hurt to inhale even a little and she wondered if Harley had broken one or two of her ribs.

Somehow she managed to drive to the house which she was now calling home easily, but sat in the car wondering what to do. She didn't know Wallace well enough to know how he would respond, but she imagined that he would call the Sheriff and there would be more trouble. At this point she didn't want any more trouble. She just wanted to be as far away from Stonewall as possible, away from Harley, away from The Barn, and away from anything that would hurt Wallace. Dear Wallace.

It was then that she noticed that Wallace was walking down the walkway towards the car. Of course. He had been waiting on her. Dear, dear Wallace. It was after midnight and he was waiting up on her like a father. Like a father. Like the father she had never had. As he approached the car he immediately knew something was wrong from the way she was sitting in the car with her head bowed.

Wallace quickened his pace and pulled open the car door. He was barely able to catch her as she passed out and slumped over into his arms. Not big or powerful, the stricken man pulled her away from the car and carried her into the house as he might a sleeping child. Laying her down on the living room floor he gasped when he saw the ugly swelling around her eye and the blood that had now been smeared all over her face. Without asking questions or needing answers, Wallace knew what had happened. It was the same thing that had happened too many times to this frail child, this young girl who had never been allowed to be a young woman. In that moment of time Wallace knew that somehow Harley would have to pay the price. Somehow, someday, somewhere, someway, Harley would suffer for hurting this girl on this night and on so many other nights.

When she finally regained her senses and realized where she was, she focused first on an anxious Wallace that was sitting beside her. She was on the floor. Sitting in the big chair was the Reverend William Lee. On the sofa sat his son, not in uniform at the moment. She struggled to get up, but Wallace gently pushed her back down. "Rest easy, girl," he said gently. "You're okay now. Nobody is going to hurt you anymore."

"It was an accident," she tried to say, but it was hard to breathe.

Reverend Lee's son, Tad, spoke. "All I need to hear you say is that it was Harley and me and the boys will bring him in, if there's anything left of him to bring in." There was anger in Tad's words and smoke in his eyes. "We don't allow men to beat up on our women in Stonewall."

Elizabeth almost wanted to laugh at his ignorance of just how many women there were like her in this small town. Most of the abuse went unreported. "I couldn't see," she said in pain. "It was dark." She gasped for air. "Didn't sound like Harley." She groaned lightly as a wave of pain hit her. "They ran away in the dark." She waited and lied one more time. "Kids I think. Punks."

No one in the room believed her nor understood why she would protect Harley. Wallace continued caring tenderly for her bruised face as an agitated Tad now strode up and down the room.

Reverend Lee finally stood and crossed over to Elizabeth. He knelt beside her and gently took her hand in his and kissing it lightly prayed silently, the only sound that of his lips striking together as he prayed fervently and hard. Finally releasing her hand he stroked her forehead. "I'm sorry, Elizabeth. If I hadn't been so hard on Harley yesterday this wouldn't have happened. I should have let Tad take him in. I am so sorry."

Finally taking a deep painful breath she murmured, "Not your fault, Preacher. It wasn't him."

Leaning in closely, Wallace looked into her eyes. "Do you want us to take you to the hospital?"

Tad chimed in quickly "I can call an ambulance." He was pulling out his cell phone when Elizabeth pushed up in a panic.

"No," she moaned. "I can't afford it. Just help me to bed and I'll be fine. I've been hurt worse."

Despite their protests the men realized that all they could do was obey her wishes. After helping her to her bed, Wallace gave her three aspirins and an ice bag before finally closing her bedroom door. Reverend Lee and son were talking lowly when he entered the living room again.

Tad spoke first. "If she won't cooperate, there's nothing we can do legally. We can start harassing him some. Giving him tickets. Writing up that motorcycle of his for not being street legal. We can't do much more than that other than threaten him." Turning to Wallace he asked "Why would she protect him? Why do they do that?"

Wallace shook his head. "She just doesn't want to cause anybody any more trouble. That's all. I'll talk to her tomorrow. At the least I'm going to ask her to quit that job at The Barn where Harley can get at her."

The minister shook his head. "Remember where we found him yesterday. Right here on your front steps. No, I think you had better insist she take out a restraining order on Harley. That will at least give Tad and the department some wiggle room in dealing with him."

It was now past 2:00 am as Wallace ushered the men out to their cars. After watching them leave, he walked quickly back to the house. He locked the front door. Worried about Elizabeth, he eased down the hall to her bedroom and stood outside her door. Opening the door quietly he heard her still crying. Almost crying himself, he sat on the floor by her bed and began stroking her head as he had Lauren's on so many nights when she had felt bad. Before long Elizabeth's crying stopped and was replaced by a heavy, labored, breathing. Wallace fell asleep with his head on the bed beside her.

Elizabeth woke several hours later to find Wallace's head beside her. Her breathing had eased, but her face and ribs still ached. Feeling her stir, Wallace sat up blinking.

"You fool," she laughed lightly, hurting as she did so. "You go on to bed."

Noting on the clock beside her bed that it was nearly 6:00 am, Wallace stood and stretched. "I need to shower and get ready for work. How are you?"

Touching the bump on her eye with her sore hand, Elizabeth winced. "Well, I've been hurt worse. Don't think I can make it to work today, though. Big Ed will fire me for sure this time."

Wallace sat down on the edge of the bed and caressed her forehead. "Listen, Elizabeth. You've got a choice to make. You either tell us the truth about Harley hurting you, or you quit that job. I can't protect you when you're there."

"Who died and made you king over me? I was fairly independent until you came along and started messing in my life." It was too early for this argument. And it did hurt to talk. Her jaw ached terribly.

Ignoring her, Wallace plunged on. "We all know that it was Harley, but if you don't cooperate, there's nothing we can do to keep it from happening again. At least if you hang out here for a while, we can keep the burglar alarm on and he can't get in without getting some help here."

"I ain't running from him. I'm sorry Wallace, but I have to live my life. In fact, it might just be better if I moved out."

"I don't have time to argue. At least for today I know you will be safe here. You can't work in that condition. We'll talk more tonight."

Wiping the curl from her forehead, Elizabeth replied "It won't matter. My mind's made up. I ain't quitin The Barn."

Stretching and yawning, Wallace simply answered "Well, you and I are in this together, like it or not, and I can be as hard headed as you." With that he left the room.

Just before he left for work, the phone rang. It was Tad Lee.

"Wallace. This is Tad. Our prayers have been answered. A call came in a couple of hours ago from Bo's Pool Hall downtown. It seems a couple of drunks got into a fight and were busting the place and each other up. Guess who one of the contestants was?"

Wallace almost shouted. "Harley? They arrested Harley?"

"Yeah," Tad answered. "But he's over at the hospital. Seems like he got whipped up worse than he whipped Elizabeth. He'll be there for a while. With his record, the judge won't let him post bail any time soon. In fact, I think somebody mentioned a parole violation. And one of our guys found a gun on Harley's bike, something convicted felons like him aren't supposed to have. Don't think we'll be seeing him around here for quite some time."

"Thanks Tad. Wait until I tell Elizabeth."

Hanging up the phone, Wallace turned to find the woman leaning against the wall in the doorway to the living room. "So they got Harley?"

"Yeah. Drunk. Disorderly. Destruction of private property. Felon carrying a concealed weapon. You don't have to worry about him anymore."

Elizabeth showed no emotion. "Then I can keep my job?" It was like a daughter asking her father.

"Yeah," the tired but relieved man answered. "You can go back to work as soon as you're able, if Big Ed doesn't fire you."

She breathed in, this time with less pain. "In that case, I'm going back to bed. And Wallace, don't be calling here all day to check on me. I'll be fine. I'll be sleeping."

It was a long morning at work for Wallace, as tired as he was, but he did wait until lunchtime to call her. "No you didn't wake me up," she responded in answer to his question. "Deputy Tad Lee called here at 8:00, 10:00 and about 5 minutes ago to see how I was doing. Reverend Lee himself called, too. I also talked to Big Ed and he's given me the week off, without pay of course. Then Momma called. And Wanda, Harley's sister called crying to apologize. So there's not been much sleep around here."

Wallace wondered at Tad. The young man had been very emotional when seeing Elizabeth hurt so badly and had sounded extremely happy that Harley had been arrested. It was just a passing thought. "Other than not getting much sleep, how are you?"

"Better, but I look like ten miles of bad road. I'm sorry you had to see me like this." A lump came in her throat so she quit talking.

"That's okay. Give it a couple of days and you will be prettier than ever." It was the first time he had told her he thought she was pretty. Elizabeth did not miss the compliment and blushed even though she was alone. He continued. "I'll see you tonight."

"I'm looking forward to it," she said, meaning it.

That afternoon, Tad called one more time as did Momma, but between their phone calls she managed to nap. She woke feeling much better just as Wallace was walking in the front door. Hearing him, she scurried to the bathroom. After taking a long, hot shower, putting on make-up to cover the bruising, and combing her hair, she felt much better. She had slept in her Waffle Barn uniform so getting into some of her new clothes helped, too. When she finally entered the kitchen she smelled supper cooking. "Hi," she called to Wallace with a smile. "Whatcha cookin?"

Surprised, the man turned around and was amazed at how beautiful she was, even with the swollen eye. "Oh, I just opened some beef stew. Something quick. Think you can eat?"

"Sure," she said, "I'm so hungry I could eat a horse."

"Good," answered Wallace. "The meat floating in this stew could be horse for all I know. Mr. Ed maybe."

"Or rat. But who cares. Just put it on some buttered bread and I'll be fine."

"So you're feeling better?" Wallace was concerned.

"I'm much better. After we eat let's go dancing. I'm up for it."

He was delighted to find her sense of humor had returned. "Maybe tomorrow night. We will go out and celebrate," he laughed. "I think we both need to go to bed early tonight."

She raised a suggestive eye to him. "Oh?"

Wallace fired a potholder across the room at her. "Don't go there."

Catching the potholder with her good hand, she tossed it back. As she left the room she called to him. "Don't you go thinking I've forgotten that kiss." He hadn't forgotten the kiss either, nor would he ever.

Chapter Eleven
When A Kiss Is Just a Kiss

"Sometimes the heart sees what's invisible to the eye."
Alfred Lord Tennyson.

It was early May and already flowers were in bloom. The bright orange marigolds that Wanda Riley had planted around her front door were the only things in the trailer park that seemed to have any color. They stood out against the drabness of their surroundings, seemingly determined to brighten their gray looking world. It made Wanda happy and proud to see them doing so well in the poor soil. Many of the surrounding trailers were faded, weather worn and barely livable. Streaks of rust running down the sides and ends of the trailers were common, bringing the only other color besides the marigolds to the yards. Yet good, honest, decent, hardworking people lived there, most proud to do so, and most did their best to keep the insides clean. Reverend Will Lee sat at a small table in the tidy trailer with Wanda across from him. Since Harley had been sent to prison for a year, Wanda was solely responsible for the rent on the trailer and it was not going to be easy on her salary.

Reverend Lee perused a list that an embarrassed Wanda had pushed across the table to him. It showed her income and her bills. The two totals did not match. "Well, Wanda," said the minister without looking up, "the church has a newly established benevolent fund set up for folks in our community that need a little temporary help. After that sermon you gave me out here the other week, I went back to the church board. We actually came out and took a tour of the area. You aren't the only one we are going to be helping." With much joy and a feeling of success in finally winning not only one, but two Waffle Barn waitresses to the Lord, the Reverend had baptized Wanda two weeks earlier. "We can do some things to help you and others." For the next hour they talked, added, subtracted, looked at the figures, talked some more and finally prayed over the list.

"I will talk to the elders who oversee the fund," Reverend Lee told her, "but I don't think there will be a problem in committing to $100 a month for the next 6 months. That will help you make ends meet, and if we get you on the food stamp program, you will make it if you are careful."

Wanda wiped away a tear. "I hate to be such a burden on the church since I'm a new member," she said lowly with head bowed. "I try so hard but just don't seem to be able to make ends meet. Now with Harley gone at least I won't be spending money on his beer."

The reverend gave her a big bear hug as he prepared to leave. "Being a member has nothing to do with us helping you. I want you to know that Wanda. I've been talking with Tad and he knows lots of folks that aren't even connected to the church that we are going to try to minister to. Our eyes have been opened the past few weeks. I've even found my way to Herbert's camp out there in the edge of the woods. Took a couple of the deacons, and their wives I might add, with me for backup, as Tad would say. It was a scary place at first, I have to tell you, but Herbert is no threat to anyone but himself. I haven't made much progress with Herbert, yet, but we are trying. Herbert told us about the locations of several other homeless folks nearby. He wants to help them even though he is resisting our efforts to get him out of there. We are taking some hot meals in right now, and we've carried some clothes. It's not much but it is a start. I'm leaning on the city council to work with us. I've also got some local business people who are more than anxious to help. Those folks in the woods may be homeless but they are still God's creatures and Stonewall citizens. Our church people are finding out that the real work of the church is outside those four walls."

Wanda noticed the smile on the big man's face. "I would volunteer to help with those folks but the good Lord knows I got enough mission work to do right here around my own front door. You've brought us all what we've been missing for a long time. Hope. We've got hope now."

"As Christians, we do have that," sighed the preacher as he was walking out. "Hebrews 6:19 says that 'We have this hope as an anchor for the soul; firm and secure."

"Thanks for that," replied Wanda. "I would like to copy that down and put on the fridge so I can see it all the time."

Reverend Lee drove away from the trailer park happy that Wanda's financial burden would be eased and that the Lord was bringing her and others the hope she had been missing. Harley would be gone for most of the coming year, but the Reverend was sure that Wanda would need her own place when Harley got out. Helping people had always excited the Will of God, but when he could see dramatic results, like with Wanda, he was thrilled. He had tried to help Harley but had been rebuffed. What saddened him was that he saw so much potential in Harley. He saw a young man who, with a little help and a lot of resolve on his own part, could be so much more, maybe even own his own garage one day. Well, you couldn't win them all. He Also knew that helping men like Harley and Herbert was a long term commitment, but the Will of God had patience because God had had patience with him.

Elizabeth MacIntosh had gone back to work at The Barn and was actually enjoying life now that Harley was gone and not a threat. She did not want to think about what would happen when he got out, so she didn't. For the first time in her life she was actually making more money than she took in and had a savings account. And two weeks ago she had been baptized the week after Wanda. Yes, things were looking up. And she had Wallace (and the Lord) to thank for it.

Since she had gone back to work, she noticed that Tad Lee had started coming by The Barn more regularly. He always sat in her area or requested her by name and he tipped very well. In fact, after a Reverend Lee blistering sermon on the subject, the waitresses at The Barn had noticed a big increase on their Sunday tips. A much impressed Big Ed was glad to see that, and was glad the local law enforcement officials like Deputy Lee were eating there because it helped keep troublemakers away. Elizabeth soon learned that Tad was just a year younger than her but had never been married. One day as she was serving him a stack of pancakes with a side of crispy bacon he asked her a question that startled her.

"Say, Mac. Just what is your relationship with Wallace? Are you sweet on him or anything? Because if you are I don't want to interfere, but if you're not and you're available, I would sure like to take you out some time."

She almost spilt the coffee all over his burly arm. "Well, no. Wallace and I are not involved or anything." She almost wished they were as she had come to respect Wallace more than any other man she had ever known or loved. Whether she was in love with him, she did not know.

"Oh," replied Tad. "Then how about it? Want to go to a movie or something? We could ride in my deputy car. I'll let you turn on the light."

She laughed. "I gotta get to work. Call me sometime."

That evening over supper Elizabeth brought the subject up with Wallace.

"Wallace, Tad Lee came by The Barn today."

Wallace looked up from his meatloaf. Among her growing list of achievements, Mac could now list cooking something more than from a can. "Yeah? How is Tad?"

98

"Well, he's been coming by The Barn all the time and today he asked if you and I were involved because if we were not, then he would like to take me out sometime."

He didn't know why nor understand it, but a sudden lump came in his throat. The shadow of the fear of loneliness once again cast a pall over him. "And what did you tell him?"

"I told him that you and I had kissed passionately on the porch so that meant we were a thing and going steady. I'm just waiting on you to give me a ring."

He dropped his fork and almost choked on his mashed potatoes. "You said what?"

Elizabeth burst out laughing. "No, I told him that there was nothing between us and he should call me sometime. I was right, wasn't I? There isn't anything between us is there? Because if there is then I can tell him." She sounded almost hopeful.

"No, No," Wallace hastened to say. "Well, we did kiss but you said it was just a kiss..."

"And we haven't kissed since then." Wallace thought he detected just a hint of disappointment in her voice.

"Right," said Wallace as he felt a flush burst across his face. Elizabeth was obviously enjoying the moment. "So you go out with Tad when he asks you and have fun and get married and raise lots of babies, just name the first boy for me."

They ate in silence for a while after that. Finally Elizabeth spoke again. "Wallace, if you were ever to want us to be involved, it would be alright. I mean I know you are older and all and that bothers you a whole lot more than it does me, because a girl like me could never ask to have any man better than you. And I really appreciate what you are doing for me. I literally have a new life."

He definitely did not want to continue this conversation. While he could have married Elizabeth and lived with her happily ever after, he knew that there was still one other woman that held a large piece of his heart and that was Rachel Lynn. He did not want to have to choose between these two. While Rachel Lynn was a tramp and a harlot and any number of other things, there was still something in her eyes that turned his head and made him want to see her. Elizabeth was everything Rachel Lynn could not hope to be, warm, loving, funny, bright, witty, but she lacked that look, those eyes, that charm that Rachel Lynn possessed. Wallace desperately wanted to love Elizabeth, but was afraid to. It would mean closing his heart to Rachel Lynn. It also meant he could be hurt again.

For her part, Elizabeth wanted to fall more and more in love with Wallace every day. She wanted Wallace and only Wallace to love her, but he was stubbornly persistent in his refusal to allow himself to do anything to encourage their relationship. Perhaps he did love Rachel Lynn too deeply, and perhaps he was afraid of being hurt again. But couldn't he try to love her just a little bit? If he cared for her as much as he said, why couldn't he allow himself to love her? A part of Elizabeth's heart ached for Wallace, ached to get close to him, ached to get him to respond to her, but no matter what she tried, Wallace rebuffed her and refused her. Perhaps the most frustrating thing was that Wallace would not let her know how he really felt in his heart about her. Maybe even more frustrating than that was the thought that Wallace might not really know.

Chapter Twelve
Shootout

"People sleep peaceably in their beds at night only because rough men stand ready to do violence on their behalf." George Orwell

It was late. A very tired Elizabeth yawned, her legs aching as they usually did after a long shift of being on her feet for hours and hours. It had been an unusually slow Friday night at The Barn with few customers and even fewer nice tips. It was these types of night when the tips were low and beer money thin, that Harley had often hammered his frustrations out on her. Now with Harley safely away in prison, Elizabeth was looking forward to her rare Saturday off when she planned on spending the day with Wallace. They were going hiking at a state park a few miles from town, an adventure that the young waitress had been excited about for weeks. The idea of spending time with Wallace out and away from their ordinary routine thrilled her. She stood dreamily at the end of the counter imagining the day they might have. It would be sunny, but not too hot, a perfect day to walk along under the shelter and shade of the huge, old hickory trees and swaying knotty pines. They would come to a hill where Wallace would turn and offer her his hand to help her climb it. She would take it, thrilling at its touch. At the top of the hill he would pull her close to him and they would kiss such a passionate but sweet gentle kiss. It was just another in a long line of activities and dreams that her new life was bringing to her. She sighed happily.

She did not see Deputy Tad Lee as he pushed slowly and quietly through the front door, but she felt his presence as it interrupted her dreams. Looking up from pouring a customer a cup of coffee, Elizabeth saw him standing there, swaying like a giant oak tree about to fall. Fear was written on his face and in his eyes. There was a small, round, ragged hole in his dirty uniform shirt and there appeared to be dried blood on one of his muscular forearms. As she looked at him, Elizabeth saw a great relief come over his face, a relief of one who has just escaped some great calamity and has come home to the one he cherishes the most to find her there waiting there patiently for him. He did not look to be a man but a small boy that wanted his mother. No words were spoken, but she knew he needed her desperately.

"Tad, are you okay?" She knew he wasn't.

Tad said no words but shook his head grimly. Intuitively, Elizabeth put the coffee pot down on the counter and stepping over to him put her arms around him, oblivious to the stares of the few customers and the two other waitresses. Tad grasped her, fighting back a complete emotional breakdown. Elizabeth looked up quickly and saw tears in his eyes as the big man began to shake, pulling her tightly to him. A moment later Big Ed eased up and touched Elizabeth on the shoulder. "I think we need to take him into my office." Gently grabbing either side of the deputy who now had large tears streaming down his face, the two helped him into Ed's crowded office and gently led him to a chair by the desk. Ed motioned for his waitress to follow him out and closed the door behind them. "I heard it on the police scanner. There was a couple of punks that held up the liquor store out near the trailer park. They tripped a silent alarm and Tad was the first one there. The kids came out shooting. Tad shot them both."

Elizabeth looked back through the dirty window at Tad who now had his head in his hands and was sobbing. "Are they….?"

Big Ed was worried. "I don't know. The last thing I heard they were in critical condition. Two kids. Just sixteen years old. Wandered over from the trailer park and had nothing better to do. They just missed killing Tad. One hit his vest, three other shots his car. He's lucky to be alive."

"But why is he here?" Elizabeth looked again back at the young man in Ed's office.

Ed looked at her with a keen, knowing eye. "Don't you know? Why do you think he keeps stopping by here and hanging around? He needs you more than anything right now. You go take care of him while I call Will of God and tell him to get over here."

Hurrying back in the office that was full of Ed's memorabilia from over the years, his awards, his pictures with celebrities that eaten there, and testimonial letters hanging on the walls, the waitress knelt in front of Tad. They said nothing for a long time as Elizabeth did not know what to say or what to do or how to comfort him. She finally took his hands from his face. Through his tears, the Deputy shook his head. "They were just kids. Kids. And I think I killed them. It was them or me, Mac! I had no choice. Maybe it should have been me lying out there instead of them." He looked to the ceiling hopelessly. There was more silence and more tears.

A grim determination filled Elizabeth as she now stood up, almost towering over the quivering man that had shrunk before her in the chair. "Tad," she said with authority. "Look at me, Tad." He refused to do so, but once again held his head in his hands.

"Tad!" she almost screamed. Tad dropped his hands into his lap to look at her, but as he did, a hand whistled through the air and smacked him sharply and meanly across the face, sending a shower of tears cascading onto the photos on the wall behind him. "Now you listen to me, Tad Lee." A shocked, stunned, bewildered son of the beloved minister stared wild eyed at this woman before him. He almost thought he saw smoke pouring out of her ears and flames from her nostrils. He shrank from what he saw.

"You listen to me, Tad, and you listen good. What you done today you done as a deputy doing his duty and not as Tad Lee. You understand that? You listening to me? You did what you were trained to do and you saved lives by doing it. If you hadn't been there some other deputy would have been and might have been killed and you would be over at the hospital crying over him right now wishing it had been you instead. Well, this time it was you but you lived. Them two boys had a choice and they made it when they picked up them guns. I hate it that they got hurt because I probably know em, but it's their fault they are where they are. Not yours. You hear me. It is not your fault. You are a good man, a good deputy, and you are going to go on being a good man and a good deputy. You hear me, Tad? And if you want to take me out sometime, you just call me and I will be proud to go out with you. You understand that? But to do that you gotta get up from here, quit your crying and get back to being the man I know you to be. So stop your sniveling and get back out there where you belong."

It was at that moment that the door behind them opened and Tad's dad walked quietly in.
Tad sniffed deeply once, wiped the back of his sleeve across his face and stood up. He looked down at Elizabeth and then to his father. "I gotta go," he said simply. "I still got work to do." He stopped to hug his dad tightly, then bent and kissed Elizabeth gently and lovingly on the forehead. With that he strode out of the office and through the crowd that was now gathered in small groups. They pushed back quickly and quietly as he passed by. One or two reached out to him to pat him on the back, some telling him how proud they were of him or thanking him. A moment later they heard his siren wailing as he went back to duty.

"You know he loves you," Will Lee said simply to the waitress as the sound faded into the distance.

"I know," whispered an emotional Elizabeth. "Now I know."

Unsettled, she realized her earlier dream might just become a nightmare.

Chapter Thirteen
"Can I Come Home?"

"Keep love in your heart. A life without it is like a sunless garden when the flowers are dead. The consciousness of loving and being loved brings a warmth and a richness to life that nothing else can bring." Oscar Wilde

"Hi, Dad. This is Lauren." It was another late Friday afternoon and Wallace was preparing to leave work. He was surprised at how depressed he was at the thought of going home, more depressed than he had been for the past few months because Elizabeth would be going out on a date with Tad. The thought troubled him. He was troubled, too for some reason, at the level of excitement he detected in Elizabeth as the event approached. She had even gone shopping by herself to buy a new outfit for the date with Tad. Wallace was watching a butterfly emerge from her cocoon and he knew from the old Elton John song if nothing else that "butterflies are free to fly, fly away…….." He didn't want Elizabeth to fly away but he knew it was inevitable.

"Hey, Lauren. I was just going to call you. Want to go with me to grab a burger or something tonight? Maybe have a fiesta at our favorite Mexican place?" He did not want to be home when Tad arrived to pick up Elizabeth. He didn't want to sit at home by himself, either, while she was gone. He imagined that he might have enough lonely nights in the future.

"Sounds great, Dad. But I need to ask you something first. Would it be alright if I moved back home?"

Wallace was thrilled at the bombshell of a question, and totally surprised. "Sure, no problem. What's going on?"

"Well, I'll tell you all about it later, but Mom and Roger are fighting all the time and I think Mom is getting ready to leave him or be kicked out. I need a place to stay over the summer and when I'm back from college on the weekends."

'Don't tell me that Roger traded his SUV for a sedan." Her father was joking but Lauren missed the humor.

"He won't let Mom drive it anymore. She had a fender bender in it. Roger treats that car better than he does us. After he got it fixed he made Mom start driving his Impala, the car his dad left him when he died. Things just haven't been the same since."

"True to form," he wanted to say, but managed to refrain. "Well," he said instead, "we'll talk about it all at supper. Meet you at the mall?"

"Sure." He could almost hear his daughter's smile. It was one of the few things she had inherited from her mother that he liked.

Late that afternoon Lauren met her father at Sears as he stared at the latest televisions that she knew he was dreaming about but could not afford, ones with huge screens and brilliant color. They wandered up and down the mall, not shopping for anything in particular but mainly just watching people go by. As the evening passed the mall began to fill up with the usual Friday night crowd, some young couples going on dates, parents dropping off or picking up their teenage children, and some people just meandering around to have something to do. Later as they sat in a back booth at the Mexican restaurant again, Lauren detailed the fights, the arguments and her growing sense that divorce was imminent between her mother and Roger. She had decided to move back home so that she wouldn't be a hindrance in that happening. "I know the situation is different, with Elizabeth staying in my old room, but I did move out on my own. That was my decision. Could I have the little bedroom at the front of the house?"

"Why don't we wait until Mac can be here to discuss this with us since she is part of the family? That would only be right."

Lauren now asked the question that was on her mind as it was on the minds of others, especially Rachel Lynn. "You said Elizabeth is part of the family. Just what part of the family is she exactly? What is going on between y'all? Are you living together, getting married or what? And where is she tonight? Working at The Barn?"

Wallace was getting tired of people asking about his relationship with the young lady but he patiently responded. "For your information and you can report this back to your mom, there is nothing going on between Elizabeth and I, just like your mom would expect, I'm sure. We are living together, but not 'LIVING' together, if you understand my meaning. There is nothing between us." His face reddened with embarrassment at having to discuss something so personal with his daughter. "And tonight she is out with Tad Lee."

"Tad Lee! That's great!" his daughter was very enthusiastic. Noticing her Dad's glum face she went on. "I mean that's great if you think it's great."

"It is truly wonderful. Tad is more her age. I'm way too old for her." He did not sound convincing as he talked and his daughter was woman enough to detect it.

"I think you're in love with her and just won't admit it. You've done a nice thing to help her out and now you don't want to ruin it by falling in love with her. And you are going to use your age as an excuse. You did take her hiking right? That was kind of like a date you know." His daughter's eyes sparkled as she poked fun at him.

"We didn't get to go. It ended up raining all day, remember? We just sat around the house watching TV. She washed clothes. I caught up on some paper work. I wouldn't call that a date."

"Oh Daddy. I think you could love her if you would just let yourself."

Wallace changed the subject. "So what will your Mom do if she and Roger divorce?"

"She will hope to get some alimony, and a new boyfriend. I bet she's already hitting the car lots shopping for a guy."

Looking at his daughter, Wallace suddenly realized that despite her mother's influence, she had blossomed into a beautiful, and increasingly wise, woman. "I couldn't have her move back home," he finally responded. "It wouldn't work anymore."

"We haven't talked about it, but I assume she could get an apartment somewhere." Lauren had really hoped that her father would try to patch things up with her mom, or at least invite her back home. Now she realized that would not happen and it saddened her because she now knew how much her father still loved her mother. Sadly, her mother had not changed and never would so she would never be satisfied living with Wallace again. Oh, she might be content for a week or a month or two, however long was convenient or that she needed to, but she would eventually find another man and Lauren knew it. It would be a man who didn't drive an old sedan.

After dinner and walking the mall some more and talking about Lauren's life, friends, boyfriends and coming year at college, Wallace escorted her to her car. As he kissed her on the forehead as he always had, she looked up into his eyes. "Daddy, if you like Elizabeth, it's okay, really. Age doesn't matter if you love someone. As much as I want Mom to come back, we both know she won't. Even if she did, she wouldn't stay long."

There was that lump in his throat again and a tear fighting to escape his eye. "What do you know about love," he finally laughed. "You're just a gull." It was the way he had always mocked the way she had said "Girl" when she was seven and missing her front teeth.

She laughed. "I'll always be your little gull, Daddy." She kissed his cheek. "Let me know when we can talk with Elizabeth about my moving back."

"Okay," he said, already feeling that unease of loneliness beginning to overwhelm him. "I'll call. But you count on moving back when you're ready."

Waving good-bye, Wallace was glad he would have Lauren back for a while. She might even be around, until she left for school, on some of these lonely nights. Facing the dark house, he allowed himself to wonder how Tad's date was going with Elizabeth. He wanted to hope that it was going well, but he couldn't bring himself to think about it any further.

Earlier that evening while Wallace had been at the mall with Lauren, Tad Lee, burly deputy though he was, a man who had courageously drawn his revolver more than once in the line of duty, a man who had been shot at and had returned fire, was terrified when he drove into Wallace's yard. He had not been on a date in a long time, and never with a woman whom he already loved so deeply. His palms were sweaty and his heart beating rapidly when he got of the car. Tad knew the moment he had fallen in love with Elizabeth had been when he had arrived here the night she had been beaten up by Harley. One look at her swollen, bruised face and his heart had melted, for even in that moment, with the bruises and dried blood still in places on her lips, she was the most beautiful creature he had ever seen. It was a strange feeling, love and rage welling up in him at the same moment, but that was how it had been. His dad had seen it, too, and knew immediately that Tad had met his life mate. He knew because he had felt the same way when he had met his wife. It was only natural, then, that Tad would go to Elizabeth when he had been involved in the shooting at the liquor store. Tad had gone just to see her that night, nothing else, just to get reassurance that somewhere in the world all was as it should be, that his gunfight may have protected one that he loved. What he had found in her was a woman that had literally knocked some sense back into him. Fortunately for everyone, both boys survived though they now faced many years in prison.

Elizabeth had been amazed that Tad would be interested in her. He was the son of a minister, a respected deputy in the Sheriff's department; a man that everyone liked more than his father, if that was possible. Tad could have had his pick of respectable women in the town and indeed several waitresses at The Barn had been jealous of his attentions towards her. She didn't deserve his attention, not with her background, not with her history of being such a loser and being with losers. In fact, she didn't deserve any of the great things that had happened to her since 'Dear Wallace' had picked her up. There it was again. 'Dear Wallace'. He was dear to her, but he was also an old fuddy duddy who was bound by his own chivalrous notions that he could not love this woman who was so much younger than he. Elizabeth had wished that Wallace would love her, because she could love him, but he wouldn't. If only he would.

Before Tad reached the front step, Elizabeth was there before him, radiant even in blue jeans and a long sleeved shirt, with her short hair which was now growing out though still sporting the little curls. Her eyes sparkled as she saw him stop dead in his tracks staring up at her with his mouth open. It was almost comical, but it was a moment she would cherish. "Gosh," he muttered. "You look great." Tad was dressed in his suit pants, a light blue shirt, and a tie.

"So do you," she responded as she skipped lightly down the steps. "So are we going by the funeral home first or what?"

Tad did not catch the humor. "Oh. Did somebody die?" He was worried.

110

Elizabeth laughed lightly. "No. You silly goose. It's just that you are so dressed up in a tie and all and I'm in jeans. Should I go back in and change? Where are we going anyway? We ain't going to some burger joint I hope."

"Well," he finally laughed, loosening his tie and removing it. "No, to tell you the truth, I changed clothes 3 times before I decided to wear a tie. I wasn't sure what you would wear. I had thought we might ride over to the mall and eat at that fancy Italian restaurant."

They were in the car now and Elizabeth did not know how to tell him that she had never eaten Italian. She had always been so finicky that she was afraid to try it. "I've never had Italian," she said honestly. "But I've had Mexican. I can eat Mexican."

Tad was comfortable now. He had never eaten Italian either but had wanted to impress. "I know a Mexican place out on the Loop, Batista's, and they love me over there. They always let me eat free when I'm in uniform."

"Alright. Let's go get your uniform on, then. Got one to fit me?" She smiled again and relaxed as the deputy laughed. Being with Tad was different. It was like being with a big, goofy puppy that was so anxious to please. Yes, he was fun. She had never been able to say that about dear Wallace.

Several hours later, a very happy, but terribly in love Tad, returned Elizabeth to Wallace's. They had enjoyed a great meal at Batista's, a meal that Felipe the owner insisted on serving them himself, and as a special treat, a mariachi band had stood beside their table and played for 15 minutes. The rest of the evening Tad had just driven her around the county showing her the spots where he had been involved in various arrests, fights and other disturbances. The only mistake had been when Tad had driven into her old trailer park, a mistake that he realized as soon as he had done it, so he drove through quickly.

Elizabeth was very quiet as they drove by her now darkened trailer, not wanting to remember the struggles when she had actually lived here. It seemed like a nightmare, a nightmare that she couldn't quite put out of her mind, but desperately wanted to.

Other than that, the evening had gone great. As they sat in his car, a sensible Toyota Camry, Tad was very uncomfortable. Now that the date was ending, he did not know if he should kiss her on the lips, on the cheek, or even at all. It grew very quiet and Elizabeth sensed his struggle. She had enjoyed the evening but was not ready to kiss him, not yet. She still carried the memory of the passionate, momentary kiss with Wallace and she did not want anything to replace it. Not yet. Not until Wallace knew for sure.

"I had a great time, Tad," she said.

She knew what he would say next but had no way to stop it. "Would you like to go out again sometime? We could do a movie or something."

She turned to him with gratitude in her eyes. She knew he loved her and always would and she did not want to hurt him. "Tad, things are little difficult right now. I'm not really sure how Wallace is with all of this."

Tad was disappointed and it showed on his face. "I understand," he said, and he did.

"Listen, Tad. I've not exactly got a spotless background ya know. I've still got more reputation to live down than you can shake a stick at. The thing about reputation, though, is that it mostly ain't true, just people talking like they assume it must be." She wasn't trying to scare him away but she did want him to know the honest, unvarnished truth right up front. "But some of what you might hear is true, so you don't deserve a girl like me. You need to be dating a homecoming queen or something. I'm not pure Tad. I've done a lot of things in my life that

I'm ashamed of now, things you've probably arrested people for. Some stuff I did out of desperation because I couldn't see no other way and other stuff I done just because everybody else was into it. I've been with people I had no business being with, but when you're caught up in that lifestyle, you just go with the crowd and don't think about right and wrong. There ain't much I hadn't done." She hung her head in shame, afraid to meet his steady gaze. "I ain't got no diseases, but it's only by the grace of God that I don't. I've done drugs and gone cold turkey to get off, the worst experience of my life. So you see, you might not want to go messing with a tarnished woman like me. I ain't got a criminal record, though I should have, but I got a terrible past. People at church are sure to talk, even more than about me and Wallace. You might run for Sheriff one day and my past could keep you from being elected. Why do you want to go out with me anyway?"

The young deputy took a deep breath before plunging into his explanation. "Well, I've always been attracted to the weak and vulnerable things in life, and you're weak and vulnerable, like a newborn fawn or one of them little baby sea turtles fighting to make it across the beach to the ocean so they can start life. In school, I was always the biggest guy in class but I always stood up for the little fellows, the kids that were always getting picked on. Once we had an autistic kid in class that everybody else picked on but he became my best buddy until they moved him to a special school. I liked him because he was so much smarter than me. He was just different, that's all."

His date smiled. "Are you saying you are attracted to me because I'm a deer, a turtle or different than everybody else?"

Tad did not return the smile but kept on talking. "When our dogs had pups I took care of the runt of the litter, the smallest one that needed some help. For some reason, maybe because I've always been so much bigger, I'm just attracted to the hurting, the powerless. I saw how

Harley had beat on you that night and I knew you needed me in your life."

Elizabeth felt a stab in her heart as she realized how much she could care for this man if she let herself. "Well, now you've compared me to a turtle and to a dog. You really know how to make a girl feel good, Tad." She laughed to show him the humor she found in it. As she said his name, another question popped into her mind. "Tad, what kind of name is Tad anyway?"

She was amused as her date went very red in the face. She almost laughed at his embarrassment. "I was a big baby, so Dad wanted a big name. They called me 'Thaddeus', which was quickly shortened to just Tad."

Strangely, the young woman did not laugh as she looked over at him. "I think Thaddeus is a beautiful name. You just don't hear it much. I think you are the first Thaddeus I've ever known." She repeated the name several times as if committing it to memory or to feel the words as they flowed over her tongue. "Thaddeus. Thaddeus . Thaddeus. I like it. What does it mean?"

Her date reddened again. "A courageous heart."

There was silence for a moment. "It fits," Mac said. "It certainly fits."

He surprised her by getting out of the car making her think for a moment that she had made him mad. As he had all evening, he walked around to her side of the car and opened the door. When she got out, Tad took her small hands in his big, tough ones. "Elizabeth," he said strongly with resolve, "I want you to understand that I don't care about your background. We all got things in our past cause we've all sinned and come short of the glory of God like Dad preached the other week. God has forgiven you for whatever past you had, so how can I hold that against you? Just remember this. I'm not going away. I will

114

always be here for you just like you were there for me when I needed you. I'm still coming over to The Barn and still hope you wait on me and will sit and talk if things are slow. Once you and Wallace sort things out, you let me know." He kissed away a tear that had rolled down her cheek. "Now you get inside before Wallace thinks we're out here necking or something."

On a sudden impulse she pushed into his arms. He towered above her and his chin rested right on the top of her head. She felt his strength and his warmth and smelled his aftershave. She hugged him tightly, then turned and hurried up the walk.

Tad stood dumbfounded for a minute, then smiled. "Old Wallace had better marry that girl," he thought, "Or I will. And I am glad she likes my name because she will be Mrs. Thaddeus Lee one day if I have anything to say about it."

Chapter Fourteen
Girl Talk

***"Love is a many splintered thing."* Anonymous**

Spring meandered into a hot summer like a slow, wooded stream and as it did, Lauren finally moved back home much to her father's delight. Mac insisted that Lauren have her old room, so Mac had moved into the smaller of the bedrooms. For the first time in her life Lauren felt like she had a sister, not a mother who wanted to be her sister, but a real sister. She could talk to Mac and Mac would understand. She opened her heart to Mac and told her things she had never told anyone. Much of their talk was giggly girl talk and often Wallace went to sleep while the girls were camped out on Lauren's bed doing their nails, brushing hair or laughing at each other, but they also learned each other's hearts, souls, and fears in talks that only girls will have with each other. Boys share their victories with each other while girls share their dreams.

One night as they were in Lauren's room chatting, Lauren detailed the breakup of her parents' marriage.

"It was fight, fight, fight all the time. Mom would go to complaining, usually about the car or the new clothes she needed but couldn't afford, and Dad would get all defensive. Then he would throw finances and charge card bills up at Mom and how much she was spending on herself. He told her once that if his mother had not bought my school clothes that year that I would have had to get on the school bus naked and my mom wouldn't care as long as she was wearing the latest fashions."

Mac nodded as she brushed a bright red polish on her toenails. "Let me guess. Your mom would holler but the louder she got the quieter your dad got, until she was doing all the hollering. Then your dad would go totally quiet after a while and leave the room. He would leave all that anger and hurt hanging in the air like all that smog in Los Angeles that I've heard about."

"How did you know?" Lauren was constantly amazed at Mac's store of wisdom.

"I know men, and I know what type your dad is."

"Is daddy a bad type of guy?" Lauren was pushing out into deep water here but she felt like she could open the subject without interfering. "Are you not interested in his type? Do you care for him at all?"

Mac sat silently for several moments before responding. "If your daddy only knew how much I do care for him. He is, without a doubt, the finest man I have ever known."

"Haven't you told him?"

"No, he won't let me." Mac stopped the nail painting and looked deeply into Lauren's eyes. "He has this notion that he is too old for me. He knows it don't matter to me but it matters a lot to him because he cares too much about what other people think and say. He feels like he did a good thing in helping me, and he did, and he feels like he would ruin it if he admitted he had fallen in love with me. People might question his motives. So no matter how long I hang around here all that will happen is that we will get older and older and never any closer in age. The other sad thing is that your dad is still deeply in love with your mother. He always will be. I can't fight that."

The younger girl hurt for her dad and believed she was feeling some of his pain. She looked at Mac with a question mark. "You mean Daddy loves both of you?"

Mac was brutally honest. "He loves me because I'm everything your mother isn't. And he loves your mother because...well....because she's

118

your mother....and because she's the first woman he ever fell so much in love with. He will always love her no matter what. He will love her till the bitter end, whatever end that might be."

"So there's no chance Daddy would ever ask you to marry him because you are competing with my mom?"

Now Mac laughed. "Honey, he would have to ask me out on a date first, and that ain't ever going to happen. People would talk... you know with him being so much older than me and me living here and all."

"And Daddy hates it when people talk about him and his business. He used to say 'What happens in this house stays in this house.' But then Mom divorced him and everyone was talking about it, especially when she married Roger the same day. He was so humiliated. Ashamed of it all. Still is. He even thought people at church were talking about him behind his back, and he was right because they were."

Mac nodded as she sat on the bed. "If it were just your daddy and me and no one else around, I think he might allow himself to love me and let me love him, but not now. It's the code he lives by. I hate that code because we do need each other."

"Is there a chance Daddy would ever take Momma back? I mean if she had nowhere else to go?"

"Not a chance the way I see it. He still loves her, but he won't let her get close again. He's too proud for that. He wants to forgive her but just doesn't know how. He knows that she will just hurt him because she has before. And she probably would walk all over him like she did when they were married."

"Hurt me once, shame on you, hurt me twice, shame on me." It was now Lauren's turn to be the philosopher.

"Yeah, something like that," Mac responded. "So you think your Mom is going to be looking for someplace to stay?" It worried Mac that Rachel Lynn might actually show up on their doorstep wanting to take up residence again. She was fairly sure that Wallace would not take her in, but Mac knew she would have to leave if Rachel Lynn did convince Wallace to allow her to come home. The thought of being forced to move back to the old trailer terrified her.

"Mom's already looking. I haven't told Daddy, but Roger's given her a month to find someplace else to live. She might not come back here but she will be asking for money. You can count on that."

Mac nodded. "And your Dad will give it to her. Even if he doesn't have it he will find some way to help her. Love is a strange thing. You find you can't live with someone, but then you can't really live without them."

"It sure is strange," laughed Lauren, "especially when you consider that a big deputy has fallen head over heels in love with a girl who barely gives him the time of day."

"Lauren," snapped Mac, suddenly sullen. "Don't go there."

"Oh, my gosh," gushed the girl as she watched the blushing face of Mac. "You are falling in love with him. You want to love my dad, but you are falling in love with Tad."

"I most certainly am not."

"But you are! Can't you see it?"

"We've been dating but it's not like he's going to ask me to marry him or anything like that. He's just like a big, old dumb puppy that keeps tripping over his own ears."

"Has he given you any gifts like jewelry or candy or flowers?"

Mac, whose fingers had been absentmindedly rubbing a silver heart attached to a necklace around her neck, dropped the fingers to her lap. She remembered the flowers that had been delivered to The Barn earlier that day, not roses, not yet, but bright yellow daisies. There had been a card, too, one that had been signed "With my love, Thaddeus". Not even Wallace had given her flowers or a card like that which she could cherish as she read it night after night before going to bed. All he had given her was a new home, a car, new clothes, a new life, a chance to bloom and a chance to love and to be loved.

A confused, angry Mac jumped off the bed and stormed out of the room. She wasn't angry at Lauren, but she was angry at herself for even beginning to think that she could love any man except Wallace. Or that any man could love her. Wallace had done more for her than anyone and she was being unfaithful by allowing herself to even consider that Tad loved her. As she scurried up the hall to her room, she realized that her heart was thumping wildly…and not from her anger…but from confusion, confusion over a love she wanted and couldn't have, or a love that was waiting for her that she wasn't yet sure she wanted.

After Mac had left the room, Lauren sighed deeply. She hoped that one day when she fell in love and someone fell in love with her that it would not be as complicated a mess as the situations she was seeing all around her. Her dad loved her mother, but could also love Elizabeth if he would only let his heart be freed from her mother. Her mother loved no one but herself. Tad loved Mac. And Mac? Mac wanted to love one man but was falling in love with another. Lauren knew Mac's heart was torn, but it would not always be so. Love would win out and when it did, someone would get hurt. A sad Lauren knew who that would be.

Chapter Fifteen
Con Man's Con

"Do not be deceived: God cannot be mocked. A man reaps what he sows." Galatians 6:7 NIV

Harley Martin was a con man. He was a con as in convict, one who had been convicted of a crime, but he was also a con man in the sense that he was good at 'conning' people, deceiving them into doing things for him or into giving him money or into believing he was somebody he was not. It was 'con' as in 'conniving' or as in 'convincing'. Now that he was back in state prison, Harley decided the only way to shorten his prison sentence was to pull off his best con job yet. He had to convince the prison staff that he was finally rehabilitated and no longer a threat to anyone.

Three weeks after arriving at Hartwell State Prison, Harley began going to the Sunday morning worship service that was provided by a local Hartwell church every Sunday at 9:00 am. A preacher and two or three loyal members would come in, lead the prisoners in singing, preach and sometimes even baptize the repentant in a portable baptistery. Several of Harley's fellow prisoners might even get up and sing solos. Harley had actually attended church often as a child. His neighbors were God fearing people who carried Harley to church every Sunday but they were the only people Harley ever knew in his life who actually cared for him. The people at that church certainly had not. When they found out that he was from a poor, drunken family they had refused to even let their children play with him. When the neighbors had moved away, Harley quit going to church because no one had even come by to offer him a ride.

Harley sat in the church service now and sang the songs he knew so well from his youth. He might be a drunk, but he still had a rich, baritone voice that rose above the others. The minister soon asked Harley to sing "How Great Thou Art" and when he did, there were few dry eyes in the cafeteria where they met. The minister stayed after the service that morning to pray with Harley. The next day the chaplain of the prison had actually come by Harley's cell to visit where they read some of the Bible together and prayed. Harley was amused by the chaplain's efforts and watched cynically as the man began to call Harley to his office every day or so for more Bible study. Harley studied hard, and even began to read the Bible during the week so he could convince the chaplain that he was becoming a man of the book.

Soon, Harley began helping the preacher and his folks set up the cafeteria for worship. It was all a matter of progression. Don't do anything too fast or they will suspect you are not sincere. Take your time. Increase your efforts. Start to talk in their words, using "Praise the Lord" or "Amen". Harley did these things and then one Sunday morning with tears in his eyes he "gave his life to the Lord" and was baptized on the spot. The water was cold, and he knew some of the other prisoners were laughing at him, but it was all part of his plan. The next Sunday he arrived at the church service smiling, with his hair cut short and his face cleanly shaven. He looked like a new man. Now he began seeking the chaplain out for extra times of Bible study and even got permission to start his own Bible study in his cellblock. Harley went out of his way to help the guards and compliment them. He asked about their families and would often stop and pray with the ones that he determined to be Christians.

He watched other prisoners 'get saved' and he knew some of them were genuine, but others were no different when they got back to their cells. They were still cheats, liars and cursers. They were playing the same game, just not as well as Harley. Their hope was that if word of their conversion got back to the proper authorities, their jail time would be lessened when they went before the parole board. Harley, however, became the part even more than the men who had really repented. He was the one to break up fights and many of the younger men and newer prisoners looked to him for guidance in the daily struggles of prison life.

Big John Hawkins, a hardened career criminal who had been in prisons for more years than he had been out, smirked every time he saw the "newly saved so freshly shaved" Harley working his religion con. Big John was a tall, strongly muscular black man who at one time had been the star linebacker for his high school football team. The old story of gang involvement, drugs, and little parental guidance soon had him working his way through the youth detention centers, and eventually into adult prison. Now in his mid-forties and serving the first year of a ten year stretch for armed robbery, he was usually a loner in the prison yard, but on this morning while walking on the track he caught up to Harley who was humming some old hymn that Big John could recognize as a hymn but couldn't remember enough to put words to.

"Old Rugged Cross," he said simply, trying to remember the hymns he used to hear in church when his grandma would take him.

A wary Harley, who had never talked to Big John answered. "No, but that's close. It's one the Rev did at church yesterday. It's called 'At Calvary.' You should join us in church sometime."

Big John laughed his deep, baritone laugh. "And get saved like you? I may be many things but I ain't going to go up against the Good Lord and pretend to be something I'm not. You can't run that con on God."

Harley sped up his walk, anxious to not be seen associating with Big John. It was not part of the image that Harley wanted to get back to the Chaplain. "Then don't. They don't force you."

The unwelcomed prisoner caught the change in his tone. "Just a word of advice. When you work a con, don't over play your hand. You can fool some of the people part of the time but you can't fool them all the time. And you ain't fooling me."

"I'm not trying to fool anybody. I got saved and I'm trying to live like it."

Big John laughed again, sweat now glistening off his dark, black arms. "If you and I were to start fighting right now, what would happen to your con? We would both get tossed into solitary. And when we got out, some of my other home boys would mix it up with you if I asked. We would start complaining about you calling us racial names, and before long you would have a rep in here that you wouldn't want."

Harley stopped and stepped off onto the inside of the track. He glanced at the guard towers, then bent over as if winded. "So you are running a con on a con man?"

"No," the other convict responded. "It's called a shake-down."

"What do you want? I ain't got nothing." If Harley had had access to his snub nosed 38 that he had hidden back home he would know how to handle this.

"Well, if you ain't got nothing then that means you got something. Here's the deal, two packs of cigarettes a week and certain other items from your store account when I require it."

"Okay," Harley responded quickly. "I need to quit smoking anyway. Chaplain says it is destroying 'my temple'. But you gotta start coming to church, sit with me, and when I tell you, get saved." Harley could imagine how impressed the chaplain would be if that happened.

Big John laughed again. He had not expected this from the pale, skinny man in front of him. Maybe he had misjudged Harley.

"I done told you I ain't gonna mess with God. But I will come to your church a time or two just to make you look good, but every time I do it will cost you something from supper."

Glad to be able to get away from his fellow convict, Harley nodded. "Done. I will get you the cigarettes this afternoon. And I will see you in church Sunday."

"Fine. Just don't be expecting to dunk me in that baptistery."

As he moved away, Harley thought "Only to drown you. Only to drown you."

Several Sunday's went by, but Harley was surprised when Big John did show up for that day's worship. Sliding into the chair beside him, the big, black man leaned over with a smile. "Hamburgers for supper tonight. I'll be takin yours in payment for coming here today."

Harley just shrugged his bony shoulders. "I don't care too much for their mystery meat anyway. I had possum once. Their burgers taste like possum."

"Yeah," grinned Big John. "That what's I like about them. All that grease."

At the end of the sermon on how God's grace could reach men in the deepest, darkest places, even prison no matter the man's background or crime, Big John had left without a word. Harley was surprised at supper when Big John did not approach him for his hamburger. He was even more surprised when Big John came back to church the next Sunday, and was stunned when at the end of the next week's service Big John had crumbled into a mass of tears and "got saved". He was baptized on the spot in the prison ministry's always ready and available portable baptistery. Everyone had been suspicious at first, but Harley noted a real difference, especially when he stopped demanding cigarettes and food. Something had happened to Big John, something real and something powerful, something that scared Harley and something he couldn't understand, so he ignored it at first. He watched for the real Big John to appear, but the man was different, and that bothered Harley.

Late one afternoon the warden sent for him. Harley laughed to himself as the guard led him to the administration building, through a series of locked doors and gates. They walked across the well-kept lawn, tended by prisoners of course, up the well swept steps, steps that always seemed to have a convict on them with a broom. They went into the hall with floors that shined like mirrors, floors that prisoners actually got on their hands and knees to polish. Harley was ushered immediately in to see the warden, and was not surprised to see the chaplain there.

Warden Samantha Cosby was a young black woman on her way up in the Department of Corrections, this being her first full-time warden assignment. She knew that with her educational background that one day she would likely be the director of the state prison system. Standing beside her was the smiling, gray headed Chaplain Ambrose who was a man of conviction and a man anxious to retire and go fishing.

Harley shook their hands with many "Yes Ma'ams" and "Yes Sirs" in response to their questions asking if he was being treated properly, if the food was good, if he was happy. Deep down Harley wanted to say "No, I'm not being treated properly. You're nasty guards cuss me and push me around. No, the food is not good. It tastes terrible and usually is not even warm. And no, I am not happy because I am in prison doing time for things that aren't my fault." Outwardly, he smiled and was very positive.

When they were seated, Warden Cosby picked up Harley's file and began to read it. "Well, Harley, it looks like you have made a few mistakes in your life."

Harley bowed his head in shame. "Yes ma'am, I have and I'm truly sorry for them. Right now I'm just trying to get my life straightened out."

She nodded. She had heard it all before and thought she was a good judge of character as she could usually spot the charlatans. Harley appeared to her to be honest and sincere. "Chaplain Ambrose says that you are doing a good work here and that you are a positive influence on the younger men. That's good."

Harley kept his head bowed in humility. "I've been here twice now, Warden, and if I can say or do something to keep other folks from making the same mistakes, then that is what I want to do."

The old chaplain spoke up. "We've heard and seen what happened with Big John. Somehow you got him to come to church and what an influence you have been on him. We couldn't believe it when we heard he was baptized, but he's a completely different man now. Everybody is talking about the change in him."

The young warden looked directly at the prisoner in front of her. "Well, Harley, as you may or may not know, the state prison system is overflowing right now and the administration is crying out for empty beds. The wardens in prisons across the state have been asked to identify prisoners who might qualify for early release. I think you have shown that you have really changed and will be different if the state gives you another chance, especially after your work with John made such a difference. That's really what caught my attention. Are you ready for that chance?"

Deep within himself he smirked and thought "Fool." The chaplain was surprised to hear his reply. 'I don't know, Warden. Oh, I won't get into any more trouble. Alcohol is my problem and when I get out I'm going straight to AA, but right now I seem to be doing more good in here with the other guys. I helped my friend, John. Maybe God needs me here to help someone else."

The chaplain spoke up again, loudly this time. "Harley! The Lord is answering your prayers. He's heard your pleas and has forgiven you and is giving you this wonderful chance to get your new life started.

Take it man! Don't throw the answers to your prayers back into God's face! God has chosen Big John to replace your Godly influence here. He can use John now and you can be free to witness on those on the outside to keep them from coming here in the first place."

"I've never heard a prisoner refuse a pardon." It was the warden with words that surprised even Harley.

He raised his head. "Pardon? Not parole?"

The Warden smiled and shook her head. "No. This is a one-time effort to make room in our prisons and we don't need to increase the work loads of our parole officers, so a small group of select prisoners will be completely pardoned by the Governor. I am recommending you, Harley. Congratulations."

Harley finally permitted himself to smile, shaking his head in disbelief. "Praise God!" the con man exclaimed, wanting to make sure he played the part to the end. "But when would I have to go?"

The young, black woman stood, and coming around her desk, hugged her prisoner. "This Friday. The pardons will be announced at noon on Friday. Chaplain Ambrose has offered to drive you home. You do have some place to live? That is very important."

"Yes ma'am. My sister, Wanda, has been living in my place while I'm gone. She got saved and is going to church and now I can't wait to get home and go to church with her. She'll be surprised." Yes, Harley grinned, Wanda really would be surprised.

"Then it's settled. You are being given a great opportunity Harley. I don't ever expect to see you back in a place like this again."

"You won't," promised Harley aloud and inside he sneered and said "You won't."

That Friday as he packed his few belongings in preparation for his release, Big John showed up outside his cell. Harley looked up at the big frame and snickered.

"I hear you been takin lessons on how to fool these folks. Well you learned from the best because I just nailed the best con job that's ever been seen in this joint. Now that you are running my con, maybe you can get released like me. But then I hear they don't usually let armed robbers out on sweetheart deals like I got.

For the last time the big man spoke to Harley. "I told you that I don't try to con God. I can only pray for those that do."

Harley stood up with a beat up duffle bag stuffed with his clothes in his hand. There was something different about John, something he didn't understand. "Don't waste your time on me. Save your prayers for somebody that it might really help."

Chapter Sixteen
Vengeance

"It takes courage to grow up and become who you really are." – E.E. Cummings

It had been nice while it lasted but Rachel Lynn never had been one to think about, much less plan for, tomorrow, so she never thought about having a long-term relationship with Roger. She had been surprised, however, when he asked her to leave because she thought things had been great up until then. If she just hadn't had that little accident in his precious luxury SUV that he thought more of than he thought of her. Now she had two weeks left to find a place, any place, to live even if it meant a woman's shelter. That limited her options. She had considered going home to old Wallace and moving back in with him, but Lauren had told her that her father was determined that Rachel Lynn was not coming back to live there. Rachel Lynn was convinced that it was because of that sweet, young, tart that Wallace had brought home. Still, Rachel Lynn was sure that if she could just spend a few minutes alone with Wallace that she would have him eating out of her hand just like she always had and dear, old Wallace would take her back. She might have to apologize and whimper a little bit and humiliate herself, and ply her womanly charms, but Wallace would cave like he always had. Yes, by nightfall she would have her old spot back until something better came along and something better always came along eventually for Rachel Lynn. She might even talk dear, old Wallace into trading that ridiculous, beat up car in for something a little snazzier. Like a fast Mustang. If he did, she might even hang around with him a little longer but only for a little while because while a Mustang would be sporty, an aging Wallace never would be. She laughed at the thought.

Two hours later an Uber driver deposited her in front of her old house. She stood there with a bulging suit case in her hand, making sure good old Wallace would take her back before getting her other possessions out of storage. As she faced the house, memories washed over her-memories of Wallace carrying her across the threshold, memories of bringing baby Lauren home, memories of playing in the yard with the toddler. Maybe she had been a fool to give it all up, but Wallace was beginning to get old and she wasn't. Oh well, she could deal with that later, too.

Hearing a loud car idling slowly down the street she turned to see a bright red 1965 Mustang roll slowly by. She liked the car. A lot. Putting on a big smile, she threw her hair back and waved lightly to the young man that was driving. He wasn't exactly handsome, but he was driving a Mustang. She saw the brake lights come on and the car backed up.

The man in the car smiled back at her. "You goin' somewhere?" he called. "I could take you there."

Rachel Lynn loved flirting. The hint of danger in it was always exciting to her. "Why, I just bet you could, if your car is as fast as you are."

The young man raced the engine and the car and ground shook. "Oh yeah, the car's fast, too. You wanna ride?"

She did not hesitate. "Sure," she called. "Mind if I throw my bag in the back?"

Harley put the car in neutral and jumped out, helping Rachel Lynn with her suitcase.
"So you comin' or goin'?" he asked.

"Both," laughed Rachel Lynn, excited to be sitting in the Mustang, feeling the revved up engine pulsing around her.

134

Getting back in, Harley raced the engine, then releasing the clutch smoked the tires for about one hundred yards, slithering this way and that, the sudden force throwing Rachel Lynn delightedly back against her seat. For the next thirty minutes Harley raced around town, only zipping up to nearly ninety miles per hour when he was sure police were not around. His companion laughed and giggled and was clearly enjoying herself. When they finally slid to a stop in front of Wallace's house, Rachel Lynn took a deep breath.

"Okay," she said gleefully, "It's my turn to drive."

The smile left Harley's face. "Sorry, my insurance won't allow that. But I tell you what. If you really like speed, we'll go out to my place and get on my Harley."

"You have a Harley Davidson! I've always wanted to ride on a Harley. Would you mind?"

"No problem," said Harley happily as he jerked the Mustang back into gear. He really liked this woman. He had never had a girlfriend older than him before, (and he assumed she was from a few wrinkles he noticed around her eyes), and never one that liked his cars. Not many minutes later they were whipping into the trailer park. They spent the rest of the afternoon riding around the town and speeding down long, open, country roads. Rachel Lynn was thrilled, thrilled at the speed, thrilled at the freedom she felt and thrilled because she was with someone who was as exciting as anyone she had ever met. She loved sitting behind him on the bike with her arms around his waist as if she had known him all her life, something that made her feel younger than she had felt in a very long time. He might not be the most handsome man she had been with, but he did have style, flash and he was younger that her, as young as she felt. He might just be worth getting to know a little better.

It was nearly nightfall when they pulled back into the trailer park. An exhausted but exhilarated Rachel Lynn got off the bike and took off her helmet, letting her hair fall around her shoulders. She had not thought about where she would be spending the night. Until now.

Harley took off his own helmet and stretched. "So you said you were comin' and goin' when I picked you up. You had your suitcase packed. What's the deal?"

Rachel Lynn took a deep breath. "Well, my husband kicked me out. I was just about to go ask my ex for a place to stay when you picked me up."

"Your ex? What's his name?"

"Wallace Harris. I was in front of our house, well, his house, when you saw me. If you will take me back out there, maybe he will let me spend the night, at least if I beg and cry hard enough."

Harley laughed to himself. He now knew that this woman was the ex-wife of Mac's boyfriend. "You can stay with me and my sister tonight. Our place is small, but we can put you up for the night and in the morning I can show you a small trailer just down the road for rent. Cheap. I know the owner. It will take a lot of work, but if Wanda helps, she's my sister, we should be able to get it livable tomorrow. It could be a nice little place for you until you get on your feet."

A trailer was a big step down for Rachel Lynn compared to where she had been living, but it was a place to live and it would give her time to sort things out with Wallace. "You sure your sister won't mind?"

Walking over to his Mustang, Harley pulled Rachel Lynn's suitcase out of the trunk. "Actually, the place is mine and she's living with me, so she don't have much of a choice. But she won't mind. She 'found the Lord' and is always trying to help save people these days. Just watch out if she goes to preaching to you."

136

Later that evening while Rachel Lynn was taking a shower, an annoyed Wanda Riley accosted her brother in the kitchen. He was sober and had not been drinking. In fact, there had not been any beer in the house since he got back from prison. "You know who she is don't you? That's Wallace Harris' ex-wife, the fellow that is helping Mac. You shouldn't be messing with her, Harley. She's nothing but trouble and will cause you nothing but trouble."

Her brother put his arm around her. "And you're supposed to be a Christian and all that good Bible stuff and are closing your door to someone in need. WWJD? What would Jesus do?"

Wanda hated it when Harley kept bringing up the Bible to her but since he had been home from prison, he had been quoting scripture to her a lot to prove his point. She did notice that he hadn't attended church with her despite her invitations. "Well, when you put it that way, I don't have a choice. But you watch yourself, Harley Martin, and don't go using her to get back at Mac and Wallace."

"Me?" Harley feigned hurt. "The thought had never entered my mind. I just want to do the Christian thing, too. Remember I was lost, but now am found, was blind but now I really see."

♦

Reverend Will Lee had to make this visit in person with news that was even more disturbing than the release of Harley from prison. Knocking on the door that still bore the scars of Harley's rock attack not so long ago, it was soon opened to reveal a smiling Wallace Harris with a glowing Elizabeth behind him. The minister was one of the few people in town that understood their relationship and did not question it. Tad was now seeing Mac often and he sensed a growing understanding between them.

After their greetings, the minister walked with them into their living room refusing to sit because of the hard news he had to share with them. He got right to the point as he had learned in life that bad news never improved with the keeping nor did it get any easier to deliver.

"I got a call from Wanda Riley this morning. She had a house guest last night."

Wallace thought he understood. "I've heard that Harley is back there."

"No, it was someone else that Harley picked up right here in front of your house. It was Rachel Lynn."

"Rachel Lynn!" Wallace was shocked.

"Wanda says that Rachel Lynn was out here planning to come up and ask you if she could stay here but then Harley drove by in that '65 Mustang he got recently. I hate to think what he was doing out here. Well, you know how Rachel Lynn is about her cars and it seems that some people like her and Harley always seem to find each other in life. Well, she and Harley hooked up somehow and she ended up spending the night with Wanda and Harley. Then they spent the day yesterday working on Mac's old trailer, fixing it up. One of Harley's buddies helped them move her stuff out of Roger's and in there. They got it looking real nice, at least nice enough for Rachel Lynn for now."

Wallace Harris felt like he had been stabbed in the back and punched in the gut. Harley was a dirty fighter, just like Mac had said, but this was beyond anything Wallace could have ever imagined. He would have preferred the pain of a real knife in the back to the horrible pain he was feeling now. And guilt. His refusal to allow her to come back had driven Rachel Lynn to this, right into Harley's arms. Now she was about to be horribly abused, beaten maybe, and certainly used by an evil man with no conscience who was out for revenge. The chain of abuse had not been broken. Rachel Lynn had just taken Elizabeth's part in it. What would Lauren do when she found out? Lauren. Would Harley now have the opportunity to get at her?

Elizabeth walked over to Wallace and held his hand. She had seen his shoulders sag and it seemed that he had aged 10 years right in front of her. As she touched him she almost felt the sadness dripping off of him. "Does Rachel Lynn know about Harley? Did Wanda fill her in?" She asked the question for him.

Reverend Lee continued pacing. He too had seen Wallace's pain. "Wanda told her, but she doesn't care. Harley's got that Mustang now and Rachel Lynn has fallen in love with his motorcycle. He's promised to get her one so they can take road trips together." The Will of God did not want to say any more, but he felt compelled to tell everything he had been told. "Rachel Lynn said she would love to have her own bike and even take Lauren for a ride. She said she's going to invite Lauren to spend the weekends with her."

Tears now welled up in Wallace's eyes and he could not stop them. "Oh, Lord! Not Lauren. Rachel Lynn is bad enough, but not Lauren."

The feeling in the pit of her stomach was growing. Elizabeth "Mac" MacIntosh knew that all of this was a result of her trying to get out of that abusive lifestyle. Harley had been right. She wasn't supposed to rise above her given station in life no matter how hard it might be. Bad things were going to happen to all the other people in her life that she had come in contact with, people that she now cared about very much. She dropped Wallace's hand. "There's only one thing to do. I've got to go back to Harley." It was plain to her.

She was shocked when Wallace turned on her with a snarl. "No!" he spit out with venom. "You. Will. Not!" The words came loudly, one definite word at a time. "We will not let him manipulate us. That's what he wants. He's not getting you back. Not now. Not ever. No way. No how!"

Mac raised her eyebrows, stunned by the sudden outburst, but relieved that she would not have to go back into that slavery. At that moment in time she loved Wallace more than she thought humanly possible. She was willing to die for him if necessary.

Will Lee now stood in front of his friend and church member, putting his hands on his shoulders as he looked into the pitifully pained eyes that were still filled with emotion. "You can talk to Lauren and keep her from going out there. She's heading off to college in a month or so anyway, so she will be safe. And you can explain the situation to her. She's got a good head on her shoulders."

Wiping his eyes, Wallace stepped back from Will Lee. "But there's still Rachel Lynn. I know she's hurt me and she's not living right, but she don't deserve what Harley will dish out. Not even Rachel Lynn deserves that. And if Harley ever lays a hand on Lauren, well, God himself wouldn't condemn me for what I'll do to Harley."

"I'll go out there myself," said the minister, "and have a word or two with Rachel Lynn, though I suspect Harley won't appreciate me hanging around there. I'll take Tad with me just in case."

Wallace Harris, feeling the initial emotion passing, pulled in a deep breath, embarrassed by his tears. "It won't help, especially if Wanda has already warned her about what kind of snake in the grass Harley is. But I guess it won't hurt much either. We have to try something."

As he drove away, heavy hearted Minister William Lee poured out his heart to God asking for wisdom in the days ahead. He was certainly going to need it.

Chapter Seventeen
Motorcycle Momma

"He degraded me in ways that I didn't even know were possible. I felt more and more worthless. As my confidence broke, he was able to convince me I was lucky to have him because no one else would want a worthless failure like me." **Adrienne Thames**

Maybe there was a God after all. Harley Martin lay in his bed with his hands locked behind his head and sighed contentedly because life was finally getting back to normal. He had his old job back at the motorcycle shop, Rachel Lynn was renting the old trailer, and once again Harley was getting ½ of that income from his friend that owned the trailer. And while Rachel Lynn was not working yet, she did have her application in down at The Barn so Harley was sure that before long he would be relieving her of some of her tip money just as he had Mac for all those years. Already she was spending her 'allowance' from her soon to be second ex-husband on Harley. No beer yet, but she did buy him some new tools that he needed. Rachel Lynn did give him some back talk from time to time but he liked that. He would tame her just as he had tamed all his other girlfriends. Yes, life was getting back to normal.

He had started drinking again even though he had promised himself in prison that he would not drink anymore once he got out. It was an expensive habit but he did enjoy the taste of beer. There was not any in the trailer when he got back because Wanda had trashed the few bottles that had been left in the refrigerator, but one night he rode by the pool hall and some of his old buddies were there. Of course, some one offered to buy him a longneck, and to be sociable he drank it, though he had to admit that it was not as good as he had remembered or thought it might be. Then he had bought the next round and before he knew it, the bar was closing and he spent the night in his Mustang in the parking lot. He knew he shouldn't have gone to the place, but he didn't have any friends that didn't drink and shoot pool. Some even did Methamphetamine, the latest drug craze. Harley was not fool enough to mess with it though he was considering an offer to distribute some on weekends when he went out on his bike.

He finally staggered home around noon, missing work completely, but then they expected that of him down at the shop. At six he woke up with what he thought was a pounding head, but was actually Rachel Lynn standing in his doorway pounding on the wall.

"Wake up," she cried. "I've tried calling you all day. What's wrong? Are you sick?"

Rachel Lynn, up until that moment, had not experienced a conversation with a hung over man. Harley sat up on the edge of the bed, still wearing his jeans but without a shirt. He massaged his head and temples, reeking of beer.

It finally dawned on Rachel Lynn that Harley had been drinking. "You're drunk," she accused. Living in that small trailer had taken some adjustment of her pride, which she had begrudgingly accepted, but she was not going to be the girlfriend of a drunk.

Harley yawned. "I'm not drunk. I was drunk and it was a great drunk. Now I'm just hung over. Get me some aspirin."

"Go get them yourself. I'm not your maid." Rachel Lynn turned around, determined to go straight back to her trailer, pack her meager belongings and get out of there. In a flash, Harley moved around the bed and before she knew it, Harley had grabbed Rachel Lynn by the neck. She tried to holler, then tried to kick him, but the immediate pain which she had never before experienced had taken her breath, and her senses, away. She struggled but to no avail as he shoved her into

142

the small kitchen and pushed her up against the sink. His beery breath stank as he leaned into her ear.

"Now get this straight," he said and the words were hard. "I told you to get me some aspirin. Don't make me get rough or I'll nail your sorry hide to the wall. Do as you're told and life will be good for both of us. You need me now, remember that, because you got nowhere else to go. Wally won't have ya and that daughter of yours thinks she's too good to be seen with ya anymore. You're a nuthin and you got nuthin but me keeping you from living in the woods or ending up in jail someday."

Very afraid, Rachel Lynn quickly found the aspirin and handed them to Harley.

"I need a drink," he said, now with less anger.

Rachel Lynn looked at him warily as she began to run water from the faucet into a glass. Harley laughed. "I said a drink. Get me a beer. Now!" His words were hard and full of a menacing threat.

Not wanting to have any more trouble, Rachel Lynn reached into the refrigerator and pulled out a beer can, one of a six pack he had brought home with him that day. She handed it to Harley then watched as he popped the top, drank half of it, took two aspirin and took another long swallow. "That's better," he said contentedly. Without a word he turned and walked back to his bedroom. The minute he was out of sight, Rachel Lynn bolted for the door and in a flash was out of it, running quickly down the street to her trailer. How had she ever allowed herself to be trapped into a relationship with a hard man like Harley and why did she stay? His words came to her as she hurried into the tiny trailer. "You got nowhere else to go"…and she didn't, but she had to get out and go somewhere else, anywhere else.

She was frantically throwing clothes into her suitcase when she heard a knock on the door. It was Harley. "Let me in," he called. "I came down to apologize. I'm sorry if I got a little rough." Rachel Lynn went over and opened the door, ready to hurl a book into Harley's face. Before she could, he stepped back and pointed to the little driveway in front of the trailer. "How do you like it? I've been working on it for you."

Behind him was a dark, shiny Harley Davison motorcycle, the one that Harley had been promising. Rachel Lynn looked at her boyfriend and a smile finally broke her face. "Mine? Really?" Harley nodded with a wide grin on his face. She almost dove down the steps into his arms, the earlier trouble all but forgotten. Her very own motorcycle. Not even Roger had done that for her. Life with Harley might not be so bad after all.

◆

"Oh Lauren, it is beautiful. You wouldn't believe it. . . Harley says I look 10 years younger when I'm sitting on it."

Lauren Harris had been listening to her mother talk non-stop for 15 minutes about the motorcycle Harley had built for her, how she had learned to ride it and now had her license. Harley even was paying the insurance for the first year. (Lauren wondered where Harley was suddenly getting so much money). The past weekend they had ridden up to visit some of Harley's friends on a lake in Alabama and had a great time skiing. When would Lauren join them?

"Mom, I don't think my going off with you and Harley would be such a good idea. I'm real busy getting ready for college and money is tight."

"Time and money. You are sounding more and more like your father every day. You need to come down here and live with me and enjoy life a little bit before you go away to school. You'd love riding behind me on my Harley."

144

Her daughter shook her head. She had visited her mom's trailer several weeks earlier and was appalled by how small it was even though Rachel Lynn kept it clean, had fresh decorations and had mostly new furniture. The first thing she had done was throw that old sofa out so Harley and one of his buddies had dumped it in pieces across the street somewhere. That had improved the smell of the place immensely, but it was still tiny and Lauren had no desire to ever visit again. Her mother was running around with a much younger man, an abuser of women, a violent drunk.

Rachel Lynn was still talking. "Harley says we can come over to pick you up and head for the beach any weekend you say. We can camp out on the sand. Wouldn't you like that?"

"Mother, really. I'm glad you're having so much fun, but I just wouldn't enjoy that."

"Harley says he might could even find enough pieces to build you a bike. Then we all three could take a trip up in the mountains and ride the Dragon's Tail. Harley says you haven't lived until you ride those mountain curves on a bike."

"Mother, I have my car. What do I need with a motorcycle? Tell Mr. Harley 'Thanks but no thanks.'"

Later that afternoon, Lauren related the conversation to her father and Elizabeth during supper. As she talked, she saw her father's face turning a deep shade of red. "But I'm not going with them. I told her that."

Wallace shook his head. "She's lost her mind. Still running around like she's a teenager. I think she got to sixteen and just quit developing. She never got over being sixteen. Fell in love with it and decided to stay there."

While Lauren started clearing the dinner plates away, Elizabeth walked behind Wallace and started rubbing his neck. "Don't let that bother you so much. Lauren and I have talked and she knows Harley for what he is. She's not going near him again. You just have to let Rachel Lynn live her own life. She may act sixteen, but she is a big girl now and has to make big girl choices."

The ringing phone pulled Elizabeth away from the job that both she and Wallace seemed to be enjoying and that Lauren had found amusing. She wondered just exactly what their real feelings toward each other might be. Then she heard Elizabeth gasp and saw a worried look cross her face as she gave the phone to Wallace. "It's Tad. He's been up at the hospital emergency room and just left. He was there trying to get a report out of Rachel Lynn. She says she fell off her bike."

Wallace jumped up and grabbed the phone. A few moments later he was running for his car with Lauren and Elizabeth behind him. As he drove he filled them in. "Tad says she showed up at the emergency room about an hour ago with her face beat up and bruises on her arm, but nothing looks to be broken. He knows Harley did it but can't prove it."

As they entered the hospital, they met a disheveled and almost drunk Harley Martin leaving. He stopped when they saw him. It was all Elizabeth could do to keep from slapping him right there in the hospital. "Hey Mac," he called out loudly. "I see you brought your boyfriend with you. Who's that cute little thing with him? Hey darling. My name's Harley. What's yours?"

From where she was standing 4 feet away, Lauren could smell the stench of beer, gasoline, and body odor. How did her mother put up with such a skunk? "You touch my momma again and you're going to find out my name is Death Angel."

Harley laughed. "Just like your momma. Full of fire and spirit. But that's how I like my women. I like to have to work to tame them, don't I Mac?"

In an instant Elizabeth crossed the short distance between them and smacked Harley hard across the cheek with the flat palm of her hand. He never felt it, and just laughed. Wallace never said a word. He simply grabbed each of the women by the arm and escorted them down the hall. As they turned the corner they heard Harley call out, "Just like your momma. I can't wait to find out for sure."

They found Rachel Lynn laying on a gurney in the hall way as she waited treatment. When she saw them, she struggled to a sitting position. "Having trouble with your Harley I hear." It was the first words Wallace had spoken since entering the hospital.

Rubbing her bruised jaw, Rachel Lynn replied "You could say that." Lauren was crying softly into Elizabeth's shoulder. The sight of her mother had been too much. Dealing with Harley Martin's mouth was one thing, but seeing her bruised and bleeding mother sitting here was hard for the young woman to handle. "I hate to ask this," said Rachel Lynn to Wallace, trying to ignore Elizabeth. "But can you take me home? I ain't staying around here. I've been here a couple of hours and haven't had an x-ray or seen a doctor or nothing. A nurse said nothing's broken but that's all they've said. Just take me home. If I'm not better in the morning, I'll go to the doctor."

Wallace answered quickly. "Okay. But you'll have to sleep on the sofa tonight."

"Not your home," snapped Rachel Lynn. "My home. The trailer. Just take me back there."

"What about Harley?" Wallace had to ask the question. It was a question he had asked a lot lately.

"He ain't your worry. He's about the only one in this world that cares anything for me right now. My own daughter won't even come to visit me."

"Rachel Lynn, we've got to get you out of that dump. I can call the Preacher and he can get some money out of his emergency fund or something and we'll put you up at a motel for the night. Or you can come home with us." Wallace was desperately searching for answers. He had shot a look at Mac when he had said it and she had immediately nodded in agreement. She knew the hell of living with Harley and would do anything to help this woman get away from that. Despite the fact that she had left him and run out on their marriage, Wallace still felt responsible for Rachel Lynn. When he had seen her on that gurney, all the old feelings had come churning to the surface. As long as he did not have to see her, he could act like she didn't exist, but whenever he did see her it was like falling in love with her all over again for the first time.

"Oh, Wallace. Stop it. I'm happy where I am for now. Just take me back there." Happy? How could she be happy with Harley around to beat her up every time he got drunk? Why would she go back to that? How could any woman go back to that life if there was any alternative at all?

Lauren wept quietly beside her mother, hating the man that had done this to her and pitying her mother. "Oh, Momma. Why do you do it? Why do you stay with him?"

Rachel Lynn sat up and pulled her daughter close for a hug. Ignoring the pain, she whispered in her daughter's ear. "He's all I got, Lauren. There's nothing or nobody else left for me."

Without another word, Wallace helped her up and without a word to any of the nurses or attendants, Wallace and Lauren helped her walk back out to Wallace's sedan. "So I get to ride in your Cadillac, again." Rachel Lynn was very adept at rubbing salt into old wounds.

As he helped her into the back seat, Wallace responded coldly and only where Rachel Lynn could hear. "Yeah, well, I might not drive a Mustang or a Harley Davidson, but I don't beat my women up."

It was a long, quiet ride back to her trailer.

Chapter Eighteen
Take A Knee

"Loneliness and the feeling of being unwanted is the most terrible poverty." Mother Teresa

Tad stood nervously in front of Wallace Harris in Wallace's living room. Elizabeth had disappeared somewhere in the back of the house. When Tad started pacing, Wallace finally spoke. "For Pete's sake, Tad, speak up. What's on your mind?" He asked, but Wallace knew why Tad was there.

With sweat pouring down the small of his back, the young deputy stopped in front of Wallace who was seated in his favorite chair. "Well, Wallace, since you've been so much like a father to her and largely responsible for us getting together, I decided to ask you. I want your permission to marry Mac, I mean Elizabeth."

There it was. Wallace had known it was coming, had hated that it was coming, but was powerless to stop it. Years of empty loneliness swelled up in front of him because he could not imagine what life would be without Mac. The past year had been full of trouble for sure, but it had been full, too, of getting Mac a driver's license, teaching her to use the internet, teaching her to cook, teaching her what it meant to live a Christian life. It had been busy teaching her so many things that she had missed, that she had never been exposed to. Yes, the year had been full and exciting. Just to come home from work and know that Mac would either be there waiting for him or would soon be home had been something worth looking forward to every day. Knowing that the house had somebody else in it at night chased away his fears of the dark. He hated to admit it, but that one solitary kiss by the door had been the highlight of the year. He could still taste her lips and smell her, just like she was that night. And now she would soon be gone.

"Mr. Harris? I mean, Wallace. It will be all right, won't it? If I ask her to marry me?"

Snapped back to reality, Wallace finally spoke. "It's her life, Tad. You have to ask her. But I think you are the best thing that's ever happened to Mac. You will be happy together. She deserves a nice guy like you after all she's been through."

Tad broke into a grin as Wallace stood and gave him a hug. "Have you and Mac talked about it? Marriage I mean?"

"Oh, sure. I haven't asked her of course, but we have looked at rings and stuff. She said I would have to talk to you before I asked her."

Sitting back down with a sinking heart, Wallace said "You have my blessing, as if it were needed." He suddenly felt very old and wondered how he would feel should Lauren ever decide to get married. "So when are you going to ask her?"

Tad flopped down on the sofa, much relieved, with a big grin on his face. "I want to get the ring tomorrow. Dad's worked out a deal with Mr. Hopkins down at the jewelry store. It's a beautiful ring. Huge rock. I'm going to take Mac over to The Barn tomorrow evening and plan to ask her right there in the first booth with all the girls there standing around. Big Ed's reserved the booth for me."

For the first time Wallace laughed. "Reservations at The Barn. I never thought I'd live to see the day."

"It's going to be a big thing. Dad and Mom are going to be in the next booth. Momma is going to come over and give her blessing. We want you there, too, Wallace, sitting with Dad."

"I had rather face an executioner," thought Wallace. To Tad he said "Sure, pal. Whatever Mac wants. It'll be great." Sighing heavily, Wallace began to contemplate a lonely future.

♦

Elizabeth knew that Tad had planned on talking to Wallace that evening. She was surprised that she was almost sorry when Tad had told her that Wallace had said "O.K." as she knew he would. Somewhere down deep in a dark, hidden, recess of her heart, Elizabeth wished that Wallace would ask her to marry him. She would have married Wallace, too, in a heartbeat. Even now, if he had asked, she would have run away to anywhere in the world he wanted, but Wallace would never give up stupid code of honor he lived by. She knew Wallace loved her. Oh, he loved Rachel Lynn and always would, but Rachel Lynn was the woman he could never have again. A dream. Elizabeth was reality. Or could have been. He would go to his grave loving them both. If only he would let her love him. Or free her to love Tad with all of her heart that she couldn't give the young deputy even now.

The next evening Elizabeth was in her best Sunday dress when Tad picked her up. Wallace had gone out earlier. As Tad pulled into the yard in his police cruiser, he saw Elizabeth standing at the top of the front stairs in that lovely blue dress that reached to her ankles. She had on a set of pearls that he had given her with matching earrings. Her hair was longer now, as long as he had ever seen it on her, and he loved it. Walking up the front steps she met him halfway, so that for once they were eye to eye as she faced him on the step above him. She kissed him tenderly.

"Wow," said Tad, totally and hopelessly in love with this beautiful creature that stood before him. "You never kissed me before a date. I kind of like that."

"So what's with the uniform?" she asked. "You taking me to that Mexican place where you get free food if you wear your uniform?"

"Oh no," he rushed to say. "I was late getting off so I just wore it. I hope it's alright."

"Sure," said Elizabeth. "Just don't go chasing any bad guys. If you plan on doing that I need to go back in and a get my weapon so I can be your back-up." They both smiled.

A few minutes later Tad surprised her by turning on his siren. They whipped into The Barn's parking lot with Tad laughing merrily. "What are we doing here?" asked a suspicious Elizabeth. "You asked me to dress up to come here?"

Tad ignored her question as he rushed around to open her door. "Come on," he said. "Ed had some customer walk out without paying earlier today. I promised I would come by and make out a report. It won't take a minute."

As they entered, the familiar smell of coffee and burned bacon accosted Elizabeth's nose and she hoped it would not attach itself to her dress so that she would smell like The Barn all night. Tad steered her toward the first booth which was empty. "Have a seat," he said. "I'll be right back."

Tad disappeared into Big Ed's office. Elizabeth sat idly looking out the window. Until dear Wallace had come along, this had been her only family. Dear Wallace.

"Elizabeth."

She turned her head to see Tad standing there with a bouquet of roses in his hands. Big Ed stood beside him on one side with a serious expression. Momma was on the other side, in her Sunday dress, wiping a tear. Suddenly from the other booth behind them popped two heads, Tad's parents. "What's going on?" she asked. "My birthday's not for another month."

There was a ripple of laughter until Tad went down on one knee in front of where she sat. Big Ed handed him a box and he opened it and presented it to Elizabeth. "Elizabeth MacIntosh, in front of these witnesses, our family and friends, I give you this ring as a token of my undying love and devotion." He now reached up and took her hand. "Elizabeth, Mac, will you marry me?"

Words that she had never expected to hear, words that she had always longed to hear, words that brought a gush of tears from eyes that had cried too much in sorrow and pain but were now crying in joy. Through the tears she saw Wallace and Lauren standing behind Big Ed. Yes, they were all here, all waiting on her to speak. Every person who meant anything to her was standing there.

It was an eternity for Tad as he knelt there in the greasy floor. Everything in The Barn had come to a standstill, except for the waitresses who were hustling up with cameras recording the scene. It seemed like it was years later, but was only a few seconds when Elizabeth responded. "Tad Lee. I would be honored to be your wife." A roar of clapping and cheers erupted as Tad gently placed the huge diamond ring on her finger. Slipping out of the booth, she stood on her tiptoes and kissed him long and hard. There were more cheers and tears. Lauren pushed through and hugged her.

Momma flopped into the booth fanning her face. "Lawd, Lawd," she moaned. "I dun warned ya about men. But ya wouldn't listen. Before long there's gonna be a bunch a little Tadpoles running around here." There was more laughter.

As the crowd thinned and folks began to get back to their meals, Wallace stepped up and shook Tad's hand and patted him on the back. His heart ached as he turned to Mac not knowing what to say or do as he fought to keep back tears, tears of fear for the coming loneliness. Mac had no idea how much he would miss her.

Mac stepped close to him and kissed him gently on the cheek and whispered quickly into his ear. "I'd still go with you. Anytime. Anywhere. Right now if you say." She really did love Tad, but she loved Wallace, too, and owed him so much. If it weren't for him and his caring about a tired waitress at the end of her shift, she wouldn't be here. The Will of God now stepped in and kissed his future daughter-in-law on the cheek. Wallace faded back into the crowd as other waitresses fought to get to their friend to congratulate her.

At the door, Wallace turned around for one more look at the radiant Mac who looked so happy. Well, she deserved some happiness in her life and Tad would guarantee she would be happy. Out in the parking lot a very lonely Wallace watched despondently as Lauren drove away to spend the night with a girlfriend. He was walking to his car when he heard a motorcycle cough a time or two, and finally crank. He knew that bike. Turning he saw the motorcycle coming towards him. It stopped.

The riders took off their helmets. "Well, well," laughed Rachel Lynn. "Looks like you lose out again. Glad I heard about all this while I was here at work today. For some reason I didn't get an official invitation."

"Don't take it so hard," grinned Harley. "Love'em and lose'em. That's life old boy." He was relishing the moment. "Thanks to you old man, I traded up. I traded a girl like Mac for a real woman like Rachel Lynn here. You got any more women stashed out at your place that I need to know about? Oh, I almost forgot about your daughter. I've been trying to meet her again."

Rachel Lynn slapped the back of his head. "Come on Harley. Old Wallace looks like he wants to go home to his big empty house and cry in his milk. By the way Wallace, how's the old car running? I saw a worn out Chevy down at a car lot yesterday. Had 175,000 miles on it. Reminded me of you. If I had the money I would buy it for ya."

"Yeah, Old Wallace likes his cars old and his women young. Don't you Wallace?"

Fighting down a terrible urge to strangle them both, Wallace never said a word. He simply turned around and walked slowly to his car. Before he got in he heard Harley call out "Don't think you won't see me anymore Wally boy. I'll be around. Mac won't be forgettin' me either. I promise you that. We still got unfinished business that I ain't forgettin'." The motorcycle roared into the night.

Chapter Nineteen
Conversations

"Let the wife make the husband glad to come home, and let him make her sorry to see him leave." **Martin Luther**

The Will of God pushed the boat away from the dock with his foot and eased to his seat behind the steering wheel. Wallace Harris sat uneasily in the chair at the front of the small aluminum boat, a swivel seat that sat above the edge of the boat. Clutching his fishing pole with one hand and trying to hang onto the edge of his chair with the other as Will Lee cranked the outboard engine, Wallace could see that this fishing trip was not going to be fun. It had been Will's suggestion when Mac had casually mentioned to the Reverend that Wallace never went anywhere, unless with her or Lauren. He spent most evenings by himself at home, since Lauren had left for college and Mac was out most nights with Tad. Reverend Lee wanted to help his friend find a hobby he could enjoy, but he also knew that men often would open up to him when out by themselves relaxing on the lake. Wallace needed to talk to someone, to share his heart, to verbalize what he was feeling about Mac. Despite the fact that Mac's fiancé was his son, Will Lee felt he could help Wallace through these troublesome days.

The lake was a small one, shallow on one end and deeper on the other near the dam. Many times Will Lee had brought people he was counseling out to this lake and had spent many hours listening to their problems as they fished. Turning the motor off and switching on the trolling motor that he guided with the foot control, the minister picked up his own fishing pole and made an expert cast towards the shore. Wallace knew how to fish, but had not been fishing in over 20 years. It took him some time before he was able to smooth out his casts and make them go where he wanted. Will ignored the other man's inexperience and continued fishing as he guided the boat down the shoreline.

They engaged in small talk mostly, discussing the weather, things going on at church, and even discussed some delicate people issues that The Will of God was having with some of his church members. Wallace listened mostly and made few suggestions. The talk turned to baseball and when the minister told a wild story about his days on the high school team, Wallace Harris laughed politely, but again offered little help to the conversation. Not having caught any fish after the first hour, with the sun beginning to beat down on them, Will cranked the small outboard motor again and quickly guided the boat across the lake to a nice, cool shady spot. This time he gently lowered the anchor into the water. Sweating profusely when that was done, he did not pick up his fishing pole. Instead he looked directly at Wallace Harris.

"Okay, my friend. Here we are. No one else for miles around. Just me and you and the good Lord and his birds and the turtles and hopefully some fish soon. I've been doing all the talking up to now. So it's your turn. Talk."

Wallace swiveled the chair around so he would not be facing his minister and gently cast out into the water. "I'm not much of a talker. You're doing a good job of it, and I like listening to you, so you go ahead."

"Wallace, look, I won't beat around the bush. I'm a straight up guy, you know that." The minister was talking to Wallace's back, but that would have to do. At least Wallace was a captive audience and would be forced to listen to him. "I'm worried about you. Lauren's worried about you. Mac and Tad are worried about you."

Why did everyone want to talk about 'Mac and Tad' and 'Tad and Mac'? It was enough to drive him crazy. Everywhere he went he saw them together. Now Tad had started coming into the house when he brought Mac home in the evenings and spent time sitting on his sofa holding her hand. In Wallace's own house! And all the wedding talk. Mac had actually asked him to walk her down the aisle and give her away, and he had agreed. Now here he was, on a fishing trip that he had not really wanted to go on, trapped, being verbally assaulted with 'Mac and Tad.'

He finished winding his lure in and recast it. He was silent, but the Will of God was not to be so easily denied. "Wallace, I'm going to ask you a question and I want you to answer me honestly. Who do you love the most? Rachel Lynn or Mac?"

Wallace was shocked, almost moaning at the question because it hurt so badly. He didn't want to answer. How could he answer? What was the answer? He shook his head and wiped his eyes with the back of his hand, fighting to get control of his emotions. His companion sat and waited. In a voice almost too soft to hear even on the quiet lake, Wallace Harris finally spoke. "I'll always love Rachel Lynn."

"That's not what I asked Wallace. I know that. Even Rachel Lynn knows that. The question is do you love her or Mac the most?"

He wanted to be far away from there. Anywhere but stuck on a boat in the middle of a lake being tortured with foolish questions. Besides, what right did the preacher have to ask him these questions? He had encouraged Tad to date Mac, hadn't he? What did he care about Wallace? Anger long suppressed began to bubble to the surface. From his side view, Will Lee saw it and was glad.

"Are you mad at Mac for running out on you like Rachel Lynn?"

Spinning his seat around to face his friend, Wallace slammed his pole down onto the floor of the boat. "Yes, I'm mad!" His lower lip was quivering. "I'm mad at you for bringing me out here to do something I hate while I have to listen to you! I get enough of you from the pulpit on Sunday."

Will Lee was persistent. "Answer my question."

161

"I love them both! Can't you understand that?" He was now choked with emotion, almost horrified at his admission, something he had known but never confessed to anyone, not even himself. He turned back around, staring out over the water.

"You love them both, but can't have either one because they both ran out on you. Something like that what you're feeling?"

The anger had bubbled out and now was gone in a flash. Wallace quickly bottled it back up to keep it hidden in that deep and dark place of his heart that no one had ever seen until now. "Yeah, something like that." Now that it was out, only brutal honesty could save him from the horror of the great fear that was looming before him.

"So what have you been so afraid of? Why don't you tell Mac you love her?"

The anger poured out again, now in a torrent that surprised them both. He was almost shouting, rocking the boat in his violent reply. "Because... she.... might... not.... love.... me... back! Some day when I'm old she would walk out on me and leave me alone just like Rachel Lynn did and I haven't got over that yet! I'm afraid of being old and alone and dying by myself. Is that so hard to understand? Who do I love the most? I love Rachel Lynn because of the way she looks, the way her hair falls on her shoulders, the way she walks. I can never look at her without loving her. Lord, I melt every time I see her and it twists me up in knots to know she's hanging out with Harley. Yet I love Elizabeth, Mac, too, because she is kind to me and understands me and says nice things to me and she is there in the evenings....or used to be until she started seeing Tad." The anger was subsiding again and he felt ashamed that it had come out. The meek, quiet Wallace was back speaking in the whisper again, throwing up his hands helplessly as the tears now flowed freely. "All I ever wanted to do was to help her because she needed help. Lord knows I didn't want to love her. I just wanted to help her. That's all I ever wanted to do. I thought we could help each other. I could give her a place to live and

162

she could keep me from being lonely." The pathetic look brought moisture to the back of Will Lee's eyes. He would have loved nothing better than to hug his friend in that moment, but he sat quietly as Wallace continued. "I do love Mac, but I could never give her all my love, all the love she deserves. She would never have all of me like she will always have all of Tad. There would always be a little something in me that I couldn't give her, some wish or desire for Rachel Lynn. She needs more than that and Tad will give it to her."

So there it was. The preacher sat in silence another moment before picking up his fishing pole once again. "And all this time I thought you were afraid of marrying Mac because she would see that you were getting fat." It came out of nowhere, lighthearted, irreverent, comical, but needed. He didn't care if Wallace laughed or not, but much to his delight Wallace did laugh. "Ashamed for her to see you without your clothes on was how I had it figured. Guess I was wrong." They started fishing again and nothing further was said about Mac or Rachel Lynn.

◆

"It's a wedding on a shoestring," laughed Elizabeth MacIntosh as she washed dishes near the end of her shift at The Barn. Momma was standing idly behind her, taking a break from her almost non-stop cooking. "You are making the dress. Will of God is marrying us for free and it don't cost nothing for the use of the church. Big Ed and the rest of the girls are going to be handling the reception."

"Fust time in all these years The Barn will be closed..and they's closing it fo yo wedding. Girl, Big Ed didn't even close The Barn when his Momma, Miss Mabel, died. He don't close for nuthin or nobody." The black matron of The Barn shook her head in wonder.

"Rachel Lynn did offer to keep it open. Said she and Harley could run the place for a couple of hours anyway." Mac ran a sponge over a syrupy plate, dunked it back in the soap dissipated water, and scrubbed it some more.

Momma laughed her deep, guttural laugh. "And have Harley walk off with the cash register? Not Big Ed. He'd rather close first. Said records are made to be broken and reckoned this was as fine a time as any fo it to happen. He ain't bout to miss yo and Mr. Tad's weddin, neither's none of the girls. So he'll just close The Barn fo it."

Mac finished the last dish and turned around, drying her hands on a nearby dishtowel.
"Momma, can I ask you a question?"

The old lady laughed again. "I know that tone of voice. Heard it from every one of my daughters before they married and from several of my girls down here over the years. It's the 'I got a question about marriage tone.'"

The young waitress looked at the floor in embarrassment. She had no one else to ask. She didn't know where her mother was and didn't even know if she was still alive. She couldn't ask Wallace or Big Ed. This was a woman to woman question and since Momma was the closest thing to a mother she had, then she would ask her. "Well, I gotta ask somebody. What it's like being married? Will I make Tad happy?"

Momma was glad that all the girl's talk now revolved around Tad. Early on it had been all about Wallace, but she seldom heard that name anymore. Momma leaned back against the counter and flashed a smile at the young girl that she loved as one of her own. "Girl, there's good married and bad married. Yo know all about bad married as yo and Harley was so tight for a while. I don't know much bout bad married, ceptin what I seen. Now I lived good married for 43 years with my Roi. Girl, we lived to make each other happy. That's good married. Not to say you won't get mad and frustrated sometimes because sometimes a man is the most frustratin thing the good Lord ever made.

And Roi had his ways, but he was a good man and I made shore he always had something good to come home to…a warm meal, a warm chair, a warm, inviting bed with me in it. I made shore he didn't need to go chasin' no other women. I was everythin' he ever needed. I worked hard at it. And he worked hard at lovin' me. We didn't take neither one for granite." She shook her head in wonder as if it were yesterday. "Girl, he used to bring me a rose home from work. Stop by the florist and pay good money to bring me a flower. After 43 years of marriage he still brought me a flower once in a while. Every night I met him when he come in with a smile on my face. I might be holdin' a chile on my hip that was wailin', but I always met him with a smile and kissed him. And ever morning that the sun rose I got up early to cook him breakfast and I was the last thing he seed as he left, a smiling, lovin', wife. That was the last thing he seed the last day he walked out the house for the last time. Had a heart attack on the bus on the way to work. Lordy, that still hurts. But I knowed as I laid him in the grave that I made my man happy and he never so much looked at another woman cause I never gave him no reason to. And he knowed in that moment that the good Lord took im, that I still loved im."

Mac stood spellbound, breathing quietly, almost reverently, hanging on every word. Finally, when Momma had finished and was staring off into space, Mac spoke. "But how do I do that? We both work shift work. Sometimes different shifts. We might not see each other for days. Things have changed since you were married."

The black woman stepped up to Mac and gently laid her hands on Mac's shoulders. "Chile, you just hasta work at it that much harder. They's gonna be days that you gonna be layin' in bed dead tired and Mr. Tad gonna be comin' home. You'se just gonna hafta sacrifice that sleep and drag your tail up out of that bed, fix yo hair, put on makeup, look nice for him, cook for him, and tell him what a good man he is. Yo do that, and Mr. Tad gonna take real good care of you."

"What's going on back here," bellowed Big Ed as he rounded the corner and spied the two women deep in conversation. Didn't y'all read the rules? No girl talk while on duty."

Both women laughed. Mac's shift was over, so she hurried to punch out her time card. Momma returned to cooking pancakes, her mind still on a handsome black man she had cooked for so many times so long ago, still loving him, and still missing him every day that passed.

♦ ♦

"Darkness cannot drive out darkness; only light can do that. Hate cannot drive out hate; only love can do that." Martin Luther King, Jr.

Hate ran deep in Harley Martin. He didn't hate Mac now because he had once loved her or because she had left him. He hated her because she now had a real chance to be happy, some chance to have possessions that Harley would never have, and she might even have the children that he would never want. (He had not seen his own child in years and didn't care to.) He hated her because she had risen above her poverty, had broken the vicious cycle of living with a woman beater. His own mother had never been able to do that. Harley's was a vicious hatred, one that wanted to harm, to seek revenge, to tear down, to destroy. If he hated Mac, he hated Wallace Harris that much more because he had dared to offer Mac the opportunity to be somebody, to love and to be loved. Wallace had interfered where he was not wanted nor needed. He had stolen Harley's property and for that he would have to pay dearly. In fact, every time he struck out at Rachel Lynn or cursed at her, he was striking at Wallace and cursing him. He didn't love Rachel Lynn, nor she him, but in a twisted way they were using each other to get back at Wallace, to punish him, to stick a knife in and twist it. Rachel Lynn believed that if Wallace had only been half the man that Harley was that she would never have had to go looking somewhere else for satisfaction in a relationship. She loved the things Harley did for her, how he took her exciting places and did exciting things, but she hated Harley for the mean streak that was in him, the one that had been beaten into him by an alcoholic father, and the one that came out when he was drinking. She was determined to leave him, but was trapped with no place else to go and knew no way out. One quick conversation on the phone with Lauren had brought her some hope. They had been talking about Mac's marriage.

"So what's your daddy going to do when Mac leaves him? Go find him another waitress somewhere to move in and take care of him? Or is he going to talk you into coming back from school to do his wash for him?"

Lauren had ignored the bitterness in her swift, but sharp reply. "Yes, Momma. I'm hoping he might be planning on rescuing another waitress, another one from The Barn, one that lives in the same trailer that Mac did for a while."

Rachel Lynn had been stunned. "You mean you think he would take me back? I don't see that happening." She had laughed a knowing laugh.

"Well, Mom, it's what I'm praying for." It was a matter of fact answer as if it had to happen just because she had prayed for it. "My small group at church is praying for that. Every time we meet we pray that God get you out of that situation with Harley. And I've met a guy at school whose dad is a preacher and he prayed with me one night about it. You just get ready cause God is going to answer my prayer. You're coming home, Mom."

Why did she have to bring up that God thing every time they talked? Yet, it did give her hope, hope that maybe somehow she could ask Wallace to forgive her. Sometimes in the dark of the night as she lay by herself in that little trailer, she would cry, hating herself for the person she had become, hating Wallace for leaving her there, praying

167

to God sometimes that Wallace would come to her rescue, even if he came in that beat up sedan. Every day it looked more and more like a new Cadillac to her.

Why had she ever started flirting with that Roger? Indeed, she had never really stopped flirting with guys, even after she was married. It was just part of her nature she liked to think. It made her feel so young to have younger men smile at her or flirt back with her. So young. That was the key to everything in Rachel Lynn's life. She was afraid of growing old, of losing her looks, of not having men flirt with her. Approaching forty, she had panicked realizing that youth was indeed fleeting. Then Roger had come along with that big, beautiful SUV and she had allowed herself to fall for him, his money and his youth, but in the end it was all an illusion. There had been no happiness with Roger, only a momentary, physical satisfaction that was soon gone. Living with Roger everyday had turned out to be worse than living with Wallace. Dear Wallace. He was the one that had suffered the most for her fear. Somehow, someway, she had to ask Wallace to forgive her and if he did, she would spend the rest of her life dedicated to making him happy. Maybe she could send a message by Lauren or maybe Will of God would help her.

But the problem was Harley. He had begun to control her life, wanting to know her work schedule, when she was coming, when she going, who she was going to be with. Rachel Lynn lived in fear of him, of his being drunk and beating her again. She even lived in fear of what he would do if he ever found Lauren somewhere alone. At first, Harley had intimidated her with threats, then he physically grabbed her and squeezed until it hurt, and then he had started hitting her. He was becoming more and more demanding of her time. Often he would come into The Barn and sip on a cup of coffee, jealously watching how Rachel Lynn waited on her customers, making sure no one got too friendly with her or made passes at her. It was as if he was afraid another Wallace Harris might waltz in and take her away. When he was drunk, or especially when he needed a drink badly, he was a man to be feared. Oh, the sweet Harley always came out when he sobered up and there were always nice gifts, like the motorcycle or flowers or now new clothes had started coming. That was the enigma that was Harley, for she saw in him a man that could be a good, decent, honorable man, a man that had a lot to give a woman, a man that could really love a woman given the chance and a man who desperately wanted to love and be loved for who he was. He had a keen sense of humor and though he never finished high school, he retained most of what he learned from watching educational shows on television, something he enjoyed doing. Harley was no dummy. But he was an alcoholic. A mean alcoholic. Rachel Lynn desperately prayed for Wallace to be her knight in shining armor that would ride to her rescue on a white stallion, or even in that sedan, but she feared what would happen when Harley found out. If Wallace didn't rescue her, then she had nowhere else to go. That small trailer had become her home, and her cell. Harley was her jailer.

Chapter Twenty
Shots Fired

"It is a far, far better thing that I do, than I have ever done; it is a far, far better rest that I go to, than I have ever known." **Sydney Carton in Charles Dickens'** *A Tale of Two Cities*

Elizabeth and Wallace stood at the back of the church in the final moments before the wedding march was to begin. Elizabeth was in a beautiful, long, white gown that Momma had helped make. Wallace wore, for the first time in his life, a gray tuxedo. He felt foolish but he looked like Prince Charming to Elizabeth.

Surprisingly, she leaned over to him and whispered lowly in his ear. "It's still not too late, Wallace. Take me away. Right now. I'll go with you anywhere. Just say the word."

The wedding march began. Stoically, Wallace faced the front of the church much as he would face a firing squad and with the same amount of enthusiasm. He said nothing and hid the pain as he was now accustomed to doing, but inside his heart was hurting so badly he thought he was about to die right there. He had rather die than do what he must do now. He must give her away. He would never admit it to her, but he really did love her. Oh, he still loved Rachel Lynn and always would, but his love for Mac was different. It was a love that he knew could be returned, a love that wanted to protect and defend, even to the death. It was a love that would sacrifice all. He might not be the one about to mouth the words "Till death do us part" but he was certainly prepared to live it. Or die it.

Leaning over he kissed her on the ear. "Tad is your life now. Make him happy." With that, he took her arm and walked her down that seemingly mile long aisle, stupid smile pasted on his face, a face that was nothing more than a mask that was hiding immense sorrow. Elizabeth took a deep breath. She had given Dear Wallace one last chance. She had owed him that for all he had done for her, for rescuing her, for bringing her to this moment that she had never imagined would be hers. Sighing, she willfully nodded. Now she would devote the rest of her life to Tad, to being the mother of his children, to living a normal life as the days with Wallace faded to a pleasant, distant memory. In all that time together they had only kissed on the lips just that once. Dear Wallace. Dear, Dear Wallace.

All too soon the Reverend William Deveraux Lee came to the final words. "You may kiss your bride." Towering over her, Tad Lee leaned gently over his new wife and kissed her long, tenderly, lovingly. "Forever", he whispered to her when their lips parted. "Forever." Then they hugged long and hard as the audience applauded. 'The Will of God' glanced quickly over at Wallace and hurt for him. His head was bowed and his eyes closed as if in prayer.

An hour later after all the wedding pictures had been taken and the wedding party had finally arrived at the church reception hall to cut the cake, Will Lee went in search of Wallace. Not finding him anywhere in the crowd he asked one of the county deputies there if he had seen Wallace.

"Yes sir," the young man who was in uniform and officially on duty replied. "He just left a few minutes ago, just after y'all got here and cut the cake."

The minister thought he understood. He would have to go find his friend as soon as the happy couple had left the reception. Wallace was certainly a man who needed ministering to. His pain had been the only sour note for the reverend on this otherwise happy evening. Sometime later, the young deputy Ron Webster, who was spending his

172

first week officially patrolling by himself, hurried up to Tad who had been his trainer.

"Gotta go, Tad. Duty calls. I just wanted to congratulate you and your bride." He hugged Elizabeth and shook Tad's hand.

"Something up?" Tad was worried about this young man going off into the night by himself.

"Just a domestic disturbance call. Nothing I can't handle. Don't worry."

With that the young man hustled out of the building. As he got to his car, he was surprised to find the Reverend Will Lee beside him. "I heard you got a domestic call," the Reverend said. "Where?" He had a sinking feeling that he knew where it would be.

"Out at the trailer park. Some drunk's been beating his girlfriend again."

"Mind if I ride with you?" Will Lee knew who the drunk was and he thought he knew where he would find Wallace. "I know the folks over there real good. I might be able to diffuse things for you."

The young deputy was relieved. "Sure preacher. Hop in and hang on to your hat. Let's see what this old car will do."

♦

Wallace had wandered aimlessly around the church's fellowship hall idly drinking the ginger ale punch. He nibbled some peanuts. Taking the napkin with Elizabeth's and Tad's name on it he gently folded it and put it into his tuxedo pocket. Hearing the wedding party finally arrive, he later watched from a distance as they happily cut the cake. Elizabeth did look happy and more beautiful than any bride he had ever seen. It pleased Wallace to know that he had helped rescue her and to give her a decent chance at happiness, but he also knew what he had to do now. There was only one present that he could give the newlyweds, freedom, a present that he would gladly give and that would make his life have meaning and purpose. With resolve stiffening within him, he took a deep breath and looking at the glowing Mac one more time, he silently left the room.

As he drove, a vision of a high school literature class swam before him. Fleetingly, for some reason he remembered the Dickens' classic *A Tale of Two Cities* and the words "It is a far, far better thing I do than I have ever done before...." He also remembered the words of Reverend Lee's sermon that past Sunday on forgiveness. Jesus had said that to be forgiven we must forgive. That meant that for God to ever forgive Wallace for his sins, Wallace had to forgive Rachel Lynn, no matter how hard that might be. Suddenly he felt that hard place in his heart melting and it seemed that a terrible burden had been lifted from him. Forgiveness. It was the key to life. Why had it taken him so long to discover that? He actually smiled with the thought that his long nightmare was ending. Rachel Lynn might not want nor accept his forgiveness, but that would be her problem. He had forgiven her and now he had to let her know. The only problem to be resolved was Harley.

A few minutes later he was pulling into the trailer park in the beat up truck of his Dad's that he had been driving, glad that at least Rachel Lynn would not see him in that old sedan that she hated so much, determined if he ever had the opportunity to trade it for something, anything a little flashier, he would. He soon was parked in front of Rachel Lynn's little trailer. As he got out of the truck he heard a terrible argument going on inside. He heard Rachel Lynn's panicked voice, then he heard the terrible, drunken curses of Harley Martin. Rachel Lynn screamed. Reaching quickly into the glove compartment to pull out a small package Wallace ran to the door and began banging on it. He felt a strange rage he had never known before welling up in him.

174

"Harley Martin. Come out here, you coward. Quit beating on women and fight somebody your own size." He tried the door but it was locked. The argument in the trailer stopped instantly. A moment later the door was swung widely open to reveal Harley Martin standing there, shirt open, with his pistol in his hand. In the background, Rachel Lynn was on her knees in the floor, blood gushing from an awful wound over her left eye. Looking up, Wallace saw terror in her face. He did not know if it was terror for her or for him.

"Get out of here," she moaned. "Go Wallace. You don't belong here."

"Neither do you," Wallace said directly to her. "I've come to tell you that I forgive you and to take you home if you'll come. I'm sorry that I haven't come sooner. I still love you Rachel Lynn and always will. Will you forgive me for forcing you into this nightmare and for not being the man you needed and deserved?" There was no fear in his voice, only a grim determination that she would be leaving with him.

Rachel Lynn's knight in shining armor had come for her at last. He had come for her, to take her home with him. He had forgiven her and miraculously had asked her to forgive him. Despite the thrill gush of relief that this gave her, there was a desperate look on her haggard, bruised and bleeding face, a look begging him to save her but begging him to get away at the same time to save himself.

Harley Martin looked down on him with an awful malice and unforgiving contempt. He had lost Mac because of this fool. He had served time in prison because of him. Now this worthless piece of flesh thought he could waltz in here and take another woman away from him. Not likely. He raised his pistol as Rachel Lynn screamed. In that instant, before he fired, Harley had to admit that he admired this man. Harley knew he would never measure up to the giant standing before him that was Wallace Harris. This man would dare challenge him for the women he loved. No matter what happened in that next second, he knew Wallace was the better man.

In that same moment, a coolheaded Wallace was confident of two things. Either he would die, and he was fully prepared to, and Harley would be arrested for his murder. Then he would be out of everyone's life forever. Or he would kill Harley and end the threats and intimidation forever. He didn't care which. It was a win-win situation for Wallace and lose-lose for Harley no matter what happened. Either way Rachel Lynn, Elizabeth and Lauren would be free. Lauren. He only regretted that he had not told her good-bye. Maybe she would understand. Stepping to one side, Wallace raised the pistol his father had kept in the truck's glove compartment all these years, and squeezed the trigger. Shots rang out simultaneously. . As he heard the loud bang of the guns, felt the repercussion of the revolver in his hand and smelled the burning sting of gunpowder, he once again thought of 'A Tale of Two Cities'. "It is a far, far better rest I go to than I have ever known."

"Shots fired!" The frantic report came over Deputy Ron Webster's car radio. "We have reports shots fired and of a man down at the trailer park."

The siren wailed seemingly louder as the deputy mashed down on the pedal even harder. Two minutes later he whirled the car into the trailer park entrance. Reverend Lee pointed him towards Rachel Lynn's trailer where they pulled up with lights flashing. "You stay in here until I get this thing under control," he ordered the reverend. The deputy was young but he was in command of the situation. He pulled his weapon as he got out, his eyes fixed on the ground in front of the car where a woman knelt weeping over a prone figure. Suddenly, a shot rang out of the darkness. Deputy Ron Webster clutched his left leg and fell. Not thinking, just reacting, Reverend Will Lee threw his door open and rolled out onto the ground as two more shots smashed the window of the car where he had been sitting. He crawled quickly around the car to the deputy who was sitting with his back to the front tire of the car, still holding onto his pistol. Reverend Lee grabbed the gun and looked quickly over the hood of the car. He saw the black shadow of a man fleeing back up the trailer park driveway with stringy hair flowing out behind.

His heart pumping rapidly, Reverend Lee tore the injured deputy's radio away from his shirt. "Officer down!" he cried out, fighting the rising panic. "Officer down at the trailer park. We need back up and an ambulance! I repeat, officer needs help!" Throughout the county the call echoed over police radios. A stricken dispatcher was now screaming over her communications system for someone, anyone, everyone to respond. Emergency calls were placed to supervisors at home and to the chief who was on vacation. At the local doughnut shop, two horrified deputies swung off their stools, knocking their coffee to the floor in their haste as they ran from the building. It was the call every police officer feared the most. Soon, from every police jurisdiction within ten miles, police cars were speeding to the assistance of a fallen brother.

Will Lee pulled the flashlight from Webster's belt and shone it on the deputy. "Where you hit? Where you hit?" The Reverend was still fighting to keep his panic down.

"Leg," the man moaned. He grimaced as a spasm of pain rocked him.

The light revealed a gaping wound in the man's leg from which dark, blood poured. Reverend Lee yanked the pocket handkerchief from his now dirty and crumpled tuxedo and stuffed it into the hole. "Hold it," he said. "You gotta hold it." Deputy Webster nodded and held the cloth. From the radio, calls were howling from police car to police car. Sirens could now be heard crying in the distance.

Gathering his wits, Reverend Lee again looked around the front of the car to the lone woman who was still kneeling there, rocking as she held a solitary figure. The minister went into a crouch and dashed over to her. He knelt there, looking quickly around. A badly beaten and still bleeding Rachel Lynn looked up. Tears streaming down her bruised cheeks, in her lap she held the peaceful face of Wallace Harris. There were several red holes in his chest, staining the tuxedo that Elizabeth had been so proud to see him wearing at the wedding. Clutched in his left hand was the napkin from the wedding reception with Elizabeth's and Tad's names on it, the napkin Wallace still had his hand on when he had approached the trailer. It was now splattered with blood.

"He's dead," she moaned. "God, he's dead." Anger surged around the minister who still held Deputy Webster's gun. He felt Wallace's neck for a pulse. There was not one.

"Rachel Lynn!" The minister grabbed the woman's arm and shook it. "Webster's been hit. He's over behind the car. He needs your help, now." The woman looked at him through her anguish and wiping her face pulled herself up as she began to stagger to the police car. Gasping at the horror of what she saw there, she forced herself to her knees and put her hand over the officer's hand that was still on the wound.

Reverend Lee now stood. Looking down at Wallace one more time, he turned and began walking purposely towards Harley's trailer. As he turned into Harley's small yard, two police cars sped by him. An ambulance followed. "Vengeance is mine," he said under his breath. "Vengeance is mine. I will repay, saith the Lord." Suddenly, other thoughts burst into his mind. "Forgive, even as I have forgiven you." "I came to seek and to save that which was lost". "For God so loved Harley Martin he gave his one and only son to be nailed on that cross for even him." Lifting his head to heaven in a brief, silent prayer, the minister turned the knob on Harley's front door.

Back at the wedding reception, Tad had just returned to the party from changing into his street clothes as the newlywed coupled prepared to leave for their honeymoon. Several off duty deputies were still there. One was on a cell phone. Tad noticed the man's face go white. He looked at Tad in horror, then hurried over. "We gotta go. A call just came over. Officer down at the trailer park!"

Tad did not look for his bride. She was forgotten as the deputies all rushed out to their cars. Word soon spread back to where Elizabeth was slipping into her blue jeans. Lauren rushed in with the news. "Mac! Something's happened out at the trailer park. There was some kind of disturbance and shooting. Ron Webster took the call and Reverend Lee went with him. Then we just heard that there's an officer down on the scene. Tad and all the deputies are on their way there." Panic filled Elizabeth as she realized that almost everyone she cared about was at the trailer park. Then another terrible thought struck her. "Oh no! Oh no! Please tell me that your dad is still here"

Lauren sobbed. "He went out before all this started. You don't think...."

The bride pulled on her sweat shirt. "I don't know. You stay here and try to get in touch with your dad. I've got to go out there." She pushed by Lauren and scurrying out a side door was soon in Wallace's beat up sedan that she had driven to the church. Before long, she was as near to the trailer park as she could get as the increasing emergency traffic was clogging the road. She pulled into a convenience store lot and ran down and across the street to a trail she had walked many times in the dark when she had hurried to buy Harley a late night pack of beer or cigarettes. It ran through the woods, along the edge of a park and emerged just behind Harley's trailer, at a shed where Harley kept his motorcycle. She saw lots of red, flashing lights in front of the trailer. Out of breath, she quickly made her way to a back door that she had used often. Breathing a prayer, she opened it silently and crawled in. Slipping down the hallway, she peaked around the corner into the living room. She almost vomited from terror when she saw Reverend Lee lying in the floor, bleeding, but alive. Harley had his back to her as he watched out the window.

Swallowing her fear because the minister needed immediate attention, Elizabeth stepped out into the living room. Hearing her steps, Harley whirled around. He was now holding his pistol and the deputy's gun that the minister had brought in with him. Elizabeth saw animal fear all over Harley, on his face, in his jerky movements, in his eyes. She saw a pathetic desperation.

"Oh, Harley! What have you done?" There was no fear in Elizabeth now, just a sincere pity for a man who had been consumed by hatred and alcohol.

"Help me, Mac," he begged. "You gotta help me." It almost made her cry.

She knelt by the unconscious minister, seeing a bullet wound in his stomach. Immediately she put her hands on it, hoping the pressure would stop the minister's life from ebbing away. "I can't help you, Harley. All you can do is give up. They'll kill you if you don't."

There were more sirens outside. Obviously, no one yet knew that Harley was the shooter. The terrified man sank down to the floor with his back to the door. He was gasping for air.

"Everybody is after me tonight. Rachel Lynn's ex-husband shows up and shoots at me and the preacher here charges in and starts preaching at me. Told me how it wasn't too late to repent and change. Well, it's too late now. When I saw his gun I had to shoot and I nailed 'im. All I was doing was protecting myself, but I'll get all the blame." He looked at the ceiling, shaking his head as Elizabeth continued trying to save her father-in-law.

Elizabeth almost fainted. Wallace had been there?

"It's all your fault, Mac." Harley was almost sobbing now. "You shouldn't have tried to be more than you are. You're trailer trash, like

180

me. You just can't go breaking the cycle. When you do, bad things like this happen. You and me were born to be here, to live like this, to help each other, to die here, but you messed it up. You were all I had, the best I ever had, but you rurn't it. You can't change your destiny."

Elizabeth felt the reverend coming to his senses under her hands. "We've got to get him some help, Harley. If we don't, he's going to bleed to death. You can't let that happen."

Harley ignored her as he shut his eyes, trying to black out the world that was screaming at him. "If you had just stayed with me like you were supposed to, everything would be fine. But you ran off with that rich fella. Everything went downhill from there. It's all your fault, Mac."

Suddenly the panicked man stood back up. "I've got to get out of here. How did you get in?" He strode quickly up to Elizabeth and hammered her wickedly across the face with one of the pistols. She rolled across the floor and smashed into the sofa. Harley grabbed her and dragged her up, putting the barrel of one pistol between her eyes. "Now tell me how you got in here."

"Back door," she gasped. "Trail through the woods. No cops."

He pushed her savagely back with his boot. "I ought to kill ya, but I won't. Not tonight. You need to live with the fact that you killed that boyfriend you was livin' with and you killed this preacher fella too."

"Wallace? What do you mean?" She stood up quickly, almost passing out from the nausea.

Harley was already in the hall with his hand on the back door when he turned back to her. "Me and Rachel Lynn was havin' a fight and your boyfriend showed up with a gun. I'm a better shot than him. I nailed him, too. You live with that."

Elizabeth swayed in pain and sorrow as Harley slipped out of the back door. Blindly she staggered to the front door and pushed it open, falling out into the night. With heroic effort, she pulled herself up and screamed for help.

Tad was kneeling beside Deputy Webster. EMT's were working on him feverishly. Rachel Lynn stood sobbing quietly in the shadows. "Ron," he called. "Ron, tell me. What happened? Where's Dad?"

The deputy forced himself to open his eyes and look at the anxious Tad. "Ambush. Will-o-God. Took my gun."

At that moment, another deputy dashed up to Tad. "Tad, the lady there says your dad had a gun and went running up to find some guy named Harley."

A scream filled the night. Fear welled up in the young man as he began to run up the street towards Harley's trailer. "Come with me," he called to the deputy behind him. As they turned into Harley's yard, more fear hit him as he saw a familiar form sprawled in front of the door. He was amazed as he rushed to her and found it was indeed his bride.

"Will's inside," she moaned through her pain and tears. "He needs help." Laying her head gently down, Tad Lee grabbed his fellow deputy's gun and yanking the door open burst into the house in a blind rage. He saw his dad writhing on the floor, alive but bleeding and in terrible pain. Another police officer that had followed Tad into the room hit the radio on his chest. "Man down! Man down! It's Will of God. Get us some help up here. Now!"

Leaving his father in the deputy's care, Tad did a brief but thorough search of the trailer. He saw the back door hanging open and knew that Harley had escaped. Forcing himself to leave his father again, Tad dashed back through the trailer and out the front door. Elizabeth was nowhere in sight. Assuming she had been carried away by the EMT's, he would have to find her later. Right now he had to find Harley, and from the looks of things there was so much panic and disorganization that Harley might easily slip away into the crowd and disappear. No one seemed to be giving orders and there was mass confusion and fear. Quickly, Tad ran to the nearest patrol car and got on the radio. "This is Deputy Tad Lee to all units. The shooter is escaping. We've got to seal off the trailer park. He might be in the woods between the trailer and the highway."

As soon as Tad had gone into the trailer, a hurting and sick Elizabeth pushed herself up and blundered into the darkness at the edge of the yard where she collapsed once again. Wallace obviously was dead in a shootout with Harley. There was no telling how bad Rachel Lynn had been hurt. Reverend Lee, her new father-in-law, lay badly wounded in the trailer. Others, including Tad, innocent people, good people just doing their jobs could be hurt or killed. And in the midst of all the police cars and ambulances and emergency personnel, Harley would escape. But how? He was out of the trailer, but where would he go? He needed transportation. His bike. Of course. He kept it in a shed at the edge of the yard. There was no doubt that he would push it along the path she had come, and crank it somewhere away from the search teams that were forming. Almost blindly, but deadly determined, the young bride got up once again and ran out to the street. She scurried with other trailer park residents who were fleeing. Reaching the entrance to the park, she turned left and ran as hard as her hurting head would allow. She passed the last police car and was running in darkness. Several hundred yards away she heard someone trying to crank an engine. Harley trying to start his bike! And he was having problems.

Elizabeth looked back towards the police cars, desperate to get their attention, but they were too far away. Crossing the street, the young woman looked for a weapon, any kind of weapon. In the ditch she found a half rotted, now in pieces sofa that had been there since it had been thrown out when Rachel Lynn had moved in. It was the same nasty sofa that had been Elizabeth's. Kicking at it savagely and with strength she had never had before, she was able to tear part of the frame off so that she had a long piece of wood in her hands. There was no hatred in her now, just a cold, hard desire to put an end to the trouble for everyone.

Running down the middle of the road in the dark, she heard Harley swear as he fought to start the motorcycle. Stopping to get her breath, she passed Harley on the far side of the road. He was so wrapped up in starting the engine that he did not see her pass. When she was about 50 yards away, she stopped and took her place in the middle of the road. She squared her feet and planted them firmly. Harley would not get past her. Not on this night. A vision of a smiling Wallace, dear Wallace, as she had met him at The Barn swam before her eyes. Until she had met Tad, Wallace had been the only man in her life ever to care for her. He had helped her to get a driver's license. She still could feel him standing behind her as he patiently taught her to use the computer. She remembered the burned meat loafs as he taught her to cook. And the one kiss. She touched her lips with the memory of it. Tears streaked her face. Now dear Wallace was dead in all likelihood, and it was her fault. Wallace did not deserve any of the bad things that happened in his life. He was a decent, honest, caring man. Everything Harley could never hope to be. Everything Harley would never want to be.

In the woods, she heard the motorcycle finally roar to life. A headlight swung into view, moving slowly towards her as Harley fought to keep it running. When the lights picked her out in the road, Harley screeched to a stop. He was amazed to see Elizabeth standing there like some ghost or apparition. In the distance, a police car swung into motion, the officers hearing the engine start and seeing the headlight leave the woods. Looking back Harley saw them speeding towards him. He revved his engine, circled back towards the police car, then turned back again now flying full speed right at Elizabeth. She was not moving. Harley did not see the piece of wood that she held behind her.

He roared towards her intent on running her down and escaping. All the hatred he had ever felt in his life focused on her in this one moment. A sneer curled his lip as he anticipated the great rush that splattering Mac all over the pavement would bring. At the last minute, almost blinded by the approaching headlight, she stepped quickly to one side and bringing up the piece of wood swung at his head like she would have a baseball bat, with every bit of strength she had left. The jolt of wood meeting head threw her to the ground, shattering her arm. Harley was thrown off the bike and bounced down the highway, part of the old sofa implanted in his brain, held firmly by the nails on the end of the board that Elizabeth had not even realized were there. The bike skidded crazily along the road throwing a shower of sparks behind it, until it finally bounded crazily into the trees and burst into flames. "Just call me 'The Wrath of God'", she thought just before passing out.

Minutes later, Tad Lee received a radio message. "Tad. This is Simpson out here on the main road, down near the liquor store. You had better get down here quick. It's Elizabeth."

First Wallace, then Deputy Webster, then his dad. Now his wife. His wife. What a wedding night. He only hoped she was alive. Running as hard as he could, he turned out of the trailer park and saw the police lights flashing in the distance. It looked like an ambulance was already there. It might not have been the fastest 100 yard dash on record, but it was the fastest he had ever run. He stopped by the front of the police car long enough to see the EMTs working on someone in the road. Further down the road lay a body under a sheet. His heart leaped in his throat. Seeing him there, Officer Simpson, a traffic cop from a nearby city that knew Tad, hurried to him and grabbed him by the shoulders. "It's Elizabeth. She's hurt, but she'll be okay. She's got a broken arm and who knows what else, but she's okay." Tad felt his strength draining away and almost fainted as he slumped by the car. Simpson stepped over and grabbed him. "It's okay, Tad. She's alive. Come on."

Assisted by the officer, Tad hurried over to where his wife was being lifted to a stretcher. Her neck had a brace on it and her back was strapped to a board to protect it. Tad grabbed her hand and kissed it. "Elizabeth," he called through his tears. "Don't leave me. Not this way. I need you." Her eyes fluttered open.

"Tad," she breathed. "Oh, Tad." He escorted her to the ambulance. When they had put her in the ambulance, he turned to Officer Simpson.

"Who's under the sheet?"

Johnson looked deeply into Tad's eyes. "It's the suspect. Harley Martin. Your wife nailed him."

Chapter Twenty One
New Birth

"Therefore, if anyone is in Christ, he is a new creation; the old has gone, the new has come!" **2 Corinthians 5:17 NIV**

Elizabeth held the tiny, little baby boy in her arms. Tad stood by her dumbfounded at the experience he had just been through in the birth of his first son. Holding the baby up to him, the large Tad took his tiny son in his arms for the first time making the baby look that much smaller. "Hello Harris," he said. "I'm your daddy." The baby smiled once, but never blinked, staring contentedly into his daddy's eyes as if to memorize every feature.

Stepping over to the bed, Reverend Will Lee snapped yet another picture with his digital camera. "That one will be priceless," he smiled. "Tad holding his Tadpole for the first time."

Lying back tiredly, Elizabeth smiled. They had named their son after Wallace Harris just as Wallace had jokingly suggested. Dear Wallace would be proud. Dear Wallace. A momentary cloud passed over her features and as if in response, the baby began to fret. In a panic, the burly deputy handed him quickly back to his mother. "Little Harris," she whispered gently. "What stories we will have to tell you of your brave grandfather and father one day." Quiet filled the room until Elizabeth smiled again. She had been smiling since the birth just hours earlier.

There was a knock at the door, and Lauren Harris peeked in. "Hi," she called. "Can Mom and I come in?"

Will Lee strode towards the door. "Come in and see my grandson," he beamed. "He's going to be a great fisherman because I'm going to teach him."

Lauren came in and behind her, shyly at first, came Rachel Lynn. After cooing over the baby and all the proper remarks and letting the women hold the child, the women turned to leave. Reverend Lee walked with them through the hospital, keeping up a constant chatter, saying "Hello" to many doctors and nurses that he knew along the way. In the parking lot, they approached a newly painted sedan. Rachel Lynn pointed to it. "Wouldn't Wallace be surprised to know that I kept his car? I had it painted and fixed up some, but it's the same car. I feel close to him, somehow, when I drive it and these days that's important to me. I think I'll spend the rest of my life repenting for the way I treated him." She sighed deeply. "I've been so foolish." Lauren went to her and held her tightly.

Will stepped up and put a hand on a shoulder of each of the women. "Let's pray," he said. "We need to pray." In the moments that followed, Reverend Will Lee poured out his heart to his heavenly Father as he interceded for these two women. Only in prayer could Will Lee come so close to approaching the throne that he had approached that night in Harley Martin's trailer. He was convinced that it was the prayer of his congregation that had pulled him through after spending a week near death in the intensive care unit. Since then, he had prayed more than ever before. The women now felt his power of the Spirit in him and felt a calm and peace come over each of them.

"Oh, Father," he almost wept. "You have been so good to us and brought us back from the valley of the shadow of death, so now we fear no evil. We have seen life taken and we have seen life restored. We have seen your grace extended to us all through your one and only son Jesus who was nailed....nailed to that old rugged cross for our sins." As he said this, the preacher's voice quavered momentarily, but then returned strong as he finished. "So now we ask that you bless this new life we have held and beheld today, and ask that you continue to give and grant us your peace that passes alllllll understanding."

After his "Amen" there were no tears of sadness, just ones of an amazing joy. "Thanks, Will," said Rachel Lynn. "And thanks for everything you did this past year or so to pull me through."

"We've all been through a lot, Rachel Lynn. And we are all stronger and closer to God for it. I've baptized half the staff over at The Barn since that night. Even Big Ed, and that baptism took some doing as big as he is. Things like what happened at the trailer park have a way of bringing people closer to the Lord. Even preachers like me find out they were living for the praise of men and not the glory of God."

"I hear you've been spending a lot of time over at the trailer park." It was Lauren speaking.

In the past, Will Lee would have bragged loudly, but the braggadocio preacher had died when he almost bled out on the floor of Harley's trailer. He had come closer to God then, closer than he had ever been before. So now he told the simple truth. "Yeah, God's doing a great work over there through Wanda, Harley's sister. We've used her trailer as a meeting place. It's a church outside the walls of our church and it's beautiful. It's been tough and we've been dealing with a lot of addictions, but we're making progress. We've even got old Herbert into detox. He's fighting it, but at least he's trying. Teachers over at the school say they can tell a difference in the behavior and grades of the kids from the park. We ran out the druggies and the city kicked out the absentee landlords, and the others came in and fixed the place up. Yeah, God's doing a great thing there. I'm excited to be a part of Wallace Harris Park!"

"While I still have triggers and scars that will always be a part of me, I am thankful that I have once again found the girl that can light up a room just with a different kind of strength behind her. I may have turned my back on God, but he never turned his back on me. He was just waiting for me to let go and give it to him. He has given

me my testimony (as related at the front of this book) so that I can help women in these situations. God has freed me from my past, and given me freedom not just to survive, but to thrive in him. I am free from the monsters in my past." Adrienne Thames

Nailed

Other Titles by Allan B. Thames:

Destiny: When the Stars Were Young, and the World Was New

Destiny Too: Sere

Your Ever Loving Soldier Boy: Korean War Love Letters

This is the Livin': The Thames Family Travelogue

Available on Amazon

38564167R00114

Made in the USA
Columbia, SC
06 December 2018